FLIGHT TO FREEDOM

The **FLIGHT TRILOGY**

BOOK ONE
Flight to Paradise

BOOK TWO
Flight into Darkness

BOOK THREE
Flight to Freedom

Please visit author's website for current and future works.
www.coebooks.com

DEDICATION

To David and Anna for their unyielding resolve to make
good choices, pursue their purpose, and acknowledge God as
THE source of all hope.

FLIGHT TO

Freedom

A novel by
Mike Coe

ISBN-13: 978-0-61585-577-6

PRINTED IN THE UNITED STATES OF AMERICA

CoeBooks.com

"Listen for GOD's voice in everything you do, everywhere you go;
He's the One who will keep you on track."

Proverbs 3:6 (MSG)

CHAPTER 1

Southern California
August 2003

*R*yan paced the house like a caged zoo animal. The moving truck was late—thirty-four minutes late, to be exact.

David, fifteen, kept his five-year-old sister, Martha, busy in a game of hide-and-seek. Moving boxes and out-of-place furniture created the perfect landscape of mountains, caves, and tunnels for Martha to hide.

Ryan checked the digital clock on the microwave for the hundredth time—8:04 a.m.

"Where are they?" he said. "They told us seven-thirty."

Keri put her hand on his shoulder. "Be patient. We've got all day."

"They said we can count on seven to eight hours to pack the truck. That means we won't get out of here until four o'clock...and that's if they started five minutes ago. It's three and a half hours to Yuma, not counting the delay on I-5 for rush-hour traffic and the bottleneck in San Diego. We'll be lucky if we make it to El Centro...that's two and a half."

"Just remember, the kids will travel much better if they

are tired."

She doesn't understand.

"By the time we get out of here, rush-hour traffic on I-5 will be a mess."

She wrapped him in a hug, looked him in the eyes, and said, "Relax, big boy. What's a couple of extra hours...or even days going to matter? This is the beginning of a whole new life. Just think, as we drive into the night with the kids asleep, I can snuggle up to you and plan our wonderful future together. Now doesn't that sound romantic?"

Ryan smiled, amazed at her ability to always live in the present, and her special way of calming his overactive mind.

He peeked behind her at the clock on the oven—8:07 a.m. "I'm not too sure about these guys. I guess you get what you pay for. I wouldn't be surprised if they load up our stuff and head to Mexico."

"Come on Ryan, don't you think you're over doing it? They're only thirty minutes late." Keri looked around the den. "And do you really think anyone would want our twenty-year-old sofa?" She chuckled. "I don't think we have much to worry about. I mean...anything the movers steal, break or damage is long overdue to be replaced or forgotten."

"I guess you're right." Ryan turned up his coffee cup, finishing the last sip, and tossed it in a half-filled garbage bag on the floor.

Keri glanced in the den to check on the children, then said, "Do you think you'll miss living in California?"

"I haven't had time to think about it. I guess in some ways...maybe. But I know for certain it's time to leave. Regardless of what lies ahead, it will be a welcomed change after what we've been through. The more miles we put between us and California, the better. We all need a fresh start."

He loved the weather and the open, non-judgmental spirit of the people in the West, but at this time, his family needed the caring, warm friendliness of the Southern culture he remembered growing up.

The tragedy on May 29th had transmogrified their sense of normal. The children would most likely repress the horror, pushing it into some inaccessible corner of their unconscious mind, while he and Keri battled recurring nightmares for the rest of their lives. They all needed a new environment—a new life.

He and Keri agreed the hardships associated with quitting his good-paying job, uprooting their young family and moving cross-country was worth the risk. However, they were not so naïve as to believe it would be an easy transition—especially for the children. Martha would most likely have the least trouble due to her curious and outgoing nature, but as a deaf teenager, David had special needs— academically and socially.

The last two months had flown by in a flurry of activity. They coordinated a large garage sale, sold their house, sold their older car, secured a rental house in Georgia, and said good-byes to friends and neighbors. In addition, they had self-packed attempting to shave down the surprisingly high cost of the 2,000 mile cross-country move.

On the upside, Ryan's new job did not require him to travel, but on the downside, it paid much less than his airline job. Keri planned to work part-time as a nurse in a walk-in clinic located in a nearby shopping center—hopefully, only temporarily. As desperately as they needed the extra money, the children also needed their mom.

Since leaving the airline, the financial pressures had been building. With no regular paycheck, their debt had grown into a mountain of gloom. Fortunately, because of the booming real estate market, their home sold at their asking price in less than a month, but the equity from the sale was quickly sucked into the bottomless pit of needs. The moving company siphoned the first five thousand off the top, then there was a one-month deposit on the rental in Georgia, the security deposit, the utility deposits, and what seemed like an endless stream of other assorted expenses. He calculated by the time they settled into their new life, they would have burned through every dime of their savings.

They prayed their car would be up for the challenge. The odometer—recently spinning past 150,000 miles—was like the ticker on a rolling time bomb. Each mile took them closer to another expensive mechanical problem. The tires had worn to the critical final few 32nds of an inch of their remaining tread depth. After arriving in Georgia, they would need to be replaced. The brakes were beginning to squeal; a sure sign the pads were wearing out.

Keri eased up beside him. "Ryan, you are so funny. You are like a little boy waiting on Christmas."

While staring at the street, looking for the moving van, he said, "Keri, have you ever wondered what might have happened if we had made different choices? I mean, if you could live any part of your life over, what would you change?"

"You mean…like, jump in a time machine?"

"Yeah, your own personal time machine to take you to any place and time in your past. Where would you go and what would you do differently?"

"I'm not too sure I want to go back."

"How can you say that? There must be *something* you would do differently."

"Who knows…it might turn out worse instead of better. I think I'll leave the past alone."

"I can think of a couple of things I'd like to do over."

"Well, Mr. Time Traveler, where…or when…is your first stop and what would you do differently?

He gave her a puzzled look. "Are you kidding? For starters, I would have never married Emily Anderson—'the man eater'."

"I never understood what you saw in that little golddigger. The first time I met her, it was obvious she was up to no good." Keri slowly shook her head back and forth. "Men are so blind when it comes to what lies beneath the surface."

"Yeah, I should have known better."

He recalled that day on the beach in front of the Hotel Del Coronado when he first met the gorgeous Emily Anderson in her bikini. He was like a wounded wildebeest in a cage with a ravenous lioness. He had never met a woman so beautiful that had shown him that kind of attention. Her flirting techniques had obviously been honed by many years of practice. The way she used her voice, her body language, and her touchy-feely approach presented a hopeless situation due to his being hormone-charged and socially inexperienced.

If I could only go back knowing what I know now.

"I like this game," she said. "What else would you change or do differently?"

"We should have never gone to your dad's condo in New York. At that point in my life, my marriage to Emily was a disaster, and the last thing I needed was to be alone with you. Seeing you made me realize what a terrible mistake I had made."

"I remember how I didn't want that day to end."

"If you had just told me about Rex...that you were engaged...and the wedding was in a week. If only you..."

She quickly interrupted, "What about Emily? Why didn't you tell me you were having problems in your marriage? Why didn't you just tell me you still loved me? If you had, I know for a fact I would have called off the wedding."

"Really! You would have called off the wedding?"

"Absolutely! I didn't tell you about Rex because, at the time, I was afraid it would spoil the few hours I had with you."

"I wish you had told me…especially after I returned home and discovered Emily had left me."

"Well…we found each other in the end…and that's really all that matters."

He smiled. "Thankfully. But if I had the chance to live that day over again, knowing what I know now, I would not have gone to the condo. That was wrong on so many levels."

"I agree. We should have taken our lunch back to Central Park and had a picnic," she said.

He continued gazing at the street, growing more anxious with each passing minute.

Keri said, "What if you could take your time machine back to the beginning…when we were in high school? How would that turn out?"

"I'm not so sure about that one."

"What?" She scrunched her face into a pretend pout.

"If you remember, your mother had you under her spell. She's the one who 'encouraged' you to dump me. Do you really think I could have convinced you to turn against the 'puppet master'?"

"I hope you would have at *least* tried."

"Well…I guess I could have charged into your house and whisked you up on my big, white steed and galloped away into the moonlight."

Keri snuggled up under his arm. "Now *that's* what I'm talking about. My prince. My knight. My Romeo."

"Finally!" Ryan called out, "They're here!"

CHAPTER 2

Atlanta, Georgia
One year later—August 2004

The Gulfstream G550 business jet navigated the darkened taxiway at the Atlanta Hartsfield International Airport like a blind man finding his way, tapping his red-tipped cane on the ground in front of him. Low clouds and fog added a milky cataract-like veil to the night, obscuring the blue-edge lights and green centerline lights defining the asphalt taxiway. Freezing temperatures made the rain-soaked black surface a breeding ground for patches of invisible black ice.

Unlike the commercial airliners Ryan had flown, the Gulfstream G550 was the epitome of luxury and considered the most technologically advanced business aircraft in the sky. The fifty million dollar twin-engine jet was capable of carrying eight passengers on nonstop legs of nearly 6,000 nautical miles at altitudes and speeds higher and faster than most commercial jets.

From the observer's seat in the cockpit, Ryan Mitchell scrutinized the two pilots seated behind the flight controls. In these weather conditions, the thought of an emergency occurring during the takeoff roll—blown tire, bird strike, engine fire or failure—would be a life-challenging test of the pilot's skills, knowledge, and crew coordination.

With the takeoff checklist complete, the Gulfstream stood ready at the runway hold line, waiting for clearance. "November one two foxtrot, Atlanta tower, runway two seven right, taxi into position and hold."

"Position and hold two seven right, one two foxtrot," said the copilot.

The captain maneuvered the jet onto the runway. With less than 2,000 feet forward visibility, the takeoff into the black hole ahead required the faith and trust only years of experience could provide.

"One two foxtrot at the middle marker turn left heading two five zero, runway two seven right, cleared for takeoff."

"Two five zero at the marker, cleared for takeoff two seven right, one two foxtrot."

"Okay, we're cleared for takeoff," the captain said, "Checklist complete. Lights are extended and on." He eased the power levers forward, paused briefly to check the engine instruments, then pushed the levers to takeoff power.

Faster and faster down the runway the jet rumbled into the foggy darkness, straining against the pull of gravity, seeking to be free from Earth's grip.

With his left hand on the control yoke and his right hand on the power levers, the captain focused intently on the beam of light carving a path in the foggy murk. Runway edge and centerline lights blurred as the jet's speed increased. Loss of power on either engine or a blown tire before flight speed was reached would require a rapid yet smooth response from the captain to maintain control of the jet and stop it safely. The copilot crosschecked and analyzed instruments in the cockpit looking for any hint of a problem. Faster and faster they rolled—both pilots spring-loaded to react to a multitude of possible problems. Each second was critical in the event of an emergency.

At 60 knots, the copilot called out, "Power set." A few seconds later, he called, "80 knots."

Seconds prior to reaching takeoff speed, the jet jolted as simultaneous pops struck the cockpit windshield.

"Birds!" the copilot said. "We've been hit by birds!" The windshield held, but the nose of the jet yawed abruptly to the right. Fire bells and flashing, red, warning lights followed. "ENGINE FIRE! RIGHT ENGINE!"

The captain shoved hard against the rudder pedal with his left foot, bringing the jet's nose back to the center of the runway. He simultaneously chopped the power levers to idle and added reverse thrust and braking. The jet slowed...85...70...slowed more...60...45.... "Silence the bell!" the captain said, as he wrestled the jet to a complete stop using rudder pedals, brakes, and nose wheel tiller.

Stopped on the runway, the captain called out, "Engine Fire Checklist." As the copilot reached for the emergency checklist, the captain transmitted a call to the tower. "Atlanta tower, one two foxtrot has aborted takeoff and is stopped on runway two seven right. We have a fire on our right engine. We are requesting emergency equipment."

"Roger, one two foxtrot. The emergency trucks are on the way."

After completing the emergency checklist, the two pilots sat calmly, waiting.

Ryan said, "Excellent. That will finish us up for today. Let's go debrief."

Prior to their move to Georgia, Ryan had landed a job with an Atlanta-based company, Flight Tech International, Inc. (FTI), as a Gulfstream G550 simulator instructor. The FTI facility in Atlanta was one of the best of its kind in the world, specializing in corporate jet ground and flight simulator training. The company had contracts to train pilots working with Fortune 500 companies, foreign governments, and a select number of wealthy individuals who owned large private jets.

Ryan exited the simulator behind the two pilots. The captain, John Dross, turned to Ryan and said, "You ever think about getting back in the air?"

Why does every student think I'm serving a prison sentence working as a simulator instructor?

"I'm pretty happy here with FTI."

"Well, if you ever change your mind, let me know." Captain Dross slipped Ryan a business card. Dross was in his late fifties and would have been perfect as Robert Young playing the role of Jim Anderson in *Father Knows Best,* or Hugh Beaumont's character, Ward Cleaver, in *Leave it to Beaver.* His brown hair was going to gray at the temples with a handsome, if not soft-featured face. He radiated quiet authority, yet was relaxed and mellow.

Ryan glanced at the white card with black print. The first word that came to mind was 'homemade'.

MERCY FLIGHT, INC.
CAPTAIN JOHN DROSS
CHIEF PILOT
770-552-1015

Unless Ryan's customers were pilots working for well-known dignitaries, celebrities, or billionaires, he typically didn't ask about their employers. Otherwise, it was the usual chit chat about the crazy ways the "rich and famous" use their sixty-five million dollar toys to jet around the globe.

"Mercy Flight. What's that all about?" Ryan said.

"We're a nonprofit organization. We use the jets to shuttle doctors, primarily surgeons, nurses, and their teams all over the globe to perform medical procedures on people who can't afford them. In most cases these patients would die if it weren't for the benevolence of this group of unusual people."

"Nonprofit?"

"Yeah. Everything we do is completely free."

"That must take big bucks!"

"We are blessed to have been well funded by a very generous man."

"Only one man? Who was he, Warren Buffett?"

"No. He was a quiet, unknown individual. You probably have never heard of him."

"I assume he is no longer living."

"He passed away many years ago."

"He must have been an amazing man. Did you know him?"

"Yes, he and I were very close, and yes, he was an amazing man. He truly cared for others more than himself. His legacy carries on because of the group of unusual men and women that work with us. They represent every specialty in the field of medicine. When they are aboard, it feels like I'm in the presence of angels from Heaven."

"Do these people get paid?"

"That's what's so unusual about them. Although there are quite a few extremely wealthy members in the group who can afford to volunteer their services, not all of the members are wealthy. Matter-of-fact, some choose to live modest lives just so they can donate more time to our cause."

"Do you cover their expenses…like food and lodging?"

"In most cases, volunteers on the other end coordinate food and shelter for the workers by providing a host home. Although, conditions are pretty bad in some places, the workers never complain. They are passionately dedicated to what they do and more than willing to sacrifice to get the job done."

What drives a person to do this?

It all sounded "out of this world". The money it must cost to fund an operation this big was mind blowing. "What about you? Does the organization pay you? Don't tell me you work for free."

"The flight crews are treated exceptionally well. They stay in the nicest hotels with an unlimited expense account. We want the flight crews to be rested and as stress-free as possible when they fly."

"How many pilots work for Mercy Flight?"

"We have two crews per aircraft..."

"How many jets does Mercy operate?"

"Not all jets. We have three Gulfstream 550s, two Beechcraft King Air 350s, and two Sikorsky S-76 helicopters."

Ryan did the math in his head. "Twenty-eight pilots total?"

"That's right. Plus flight attendants, maintenance specialists, and assorted other support staff."

"Wow! That is quite an operation." Ryan glanced at Captain Dross's business card: 'Chief Pilot'. "Where do you hangar all these aircraft?"

"One Gulfstream, King Air, and helicopter are based at Teterboro Airport in New Jersey, the same setup on the West Coast at John Wayne Airport in Orange County, and the last Gulfstream is kept here in Atlanta at Peachtree DeKalb Airport. Our corporate office is also here in Atlanta."

"Where do you live?"

"I live up the road in Buckhead."

"Pricy neighborhood."

"Yes it is, but I'm not an owner."

"Still, I'll bet the rent is out of sight."

"Well...I'm not a renter either. It's complicated."

Ryan could tell he had pushed a bit too far into John's personal life. If he didn't own or rent, now was not the time to unwrap the word 'complicated'. "Buckhead is my old stomping ground. I grew up there."

"Where do you live now?"

"We live in a condo complex off of Pharr Road."

"I guess that makes us neighbors."

Ryan checked his watch. "I need to finish up your debrief and let you guys hit the road."

Ryan didn't have much to critique about the training ride for John and his copilot; mostly because they did an excellent job, but partly because his mind was still processing John's job offer. The idea of joining an organization like Mercy Flight was intriguing. Using his skills, talents, and experience as a part of a team doing amazing work, made him wonder if his entire journey in life might have been divinely orchestrated for this one final opportunity.

John never did answer my question about pay.

If the pay is less than what he currently made, it would definitely be a deal breaker. He and Keri were slowly whittling down their debt and had managed to buy a second car, but Keri still worked part-time and would need to continue until all of their debts were paid; hopefully, not more than a couple of years.

Leaving the briefing room, Captain Dross turned to his copilot. "Michael, we take Dr. Lang and his team to San Juan in the morning."

"Right. I'll be at the hangar by six."

"See you then."

The men shook hands and Michael rushed off. "So, Ryan, like I said, if you ever feel like you want to get back in the air, give me a call. I would love to answer any of your questions and see if we can work something out."

"I'll talk to my wife this weekend and see what she thinks."

Should I ask him about the pay?

"Sounds great! I'll be out of town this week for a few days starting tomorrow, but you can reach me on my cell regardless of where I am. Call anytime."

They shook hands and John left.

Ryan finished the paperwork and headed for the parking

lot. It was Friday and he had the weekend off. Tonight was homemade pizza and movie night at the Mitchell house. Since they'd been in Georgia, Ryan had learned to toss a mean pizza. He left the movie selection up to Keri and the kids.

The more he thought about the job at Mercy, the more excited he became. He couldn't wait to talk to Keri. If they paid him enough, she might be able to stop working.

I forgot to ask John where the job opening was located.

Moving the family to New Jersey was out of the question, and Keri would never move back to Orange County. The mere mention of returning to California would horrify the entire family.

Maybe I should wait until after I meet with John before I tell Keri.

CHAPTER 3

Buckhead, Georgia
Friday afternoon—August 2004

The drive home seemed quicker than normal. John Dross had stirred Ryan's mind into a flurry of hopeful possibilities—a new job with a unique purpose, better pay allowing Keri to stop working, and a better life for the children.

But then there were the deal breakers—moving to New Jersey; moving back to California; numerous overnight trips; less or equal pay.

He turned off Peachtree Road, onto Pharr Road, then Pharr Court. The Habersham was a gated mid-rise condo complex with 194 residential units shaded by beautiful trees, nicely landscaped, with a secure entrance to the building. Keri was initially drawn to the place because of the name being the same as the street where she had grown up. Built as a cooperative in 1961 and converted to condos in 1983, the complex was located in a safe area on the fringes of Buckhead.

"Is the pizza ready?" Ryan said, as he walked in the door.

"Hi, honey," Keri said, meeting him with a hug and a kiss. "The kids are starving. They've been asking me for hours when dad would be home."

"Keri, you won't believe what happened today at work. One of the pilots I was training…"

"Hi, daddy. I'm hungry," said Martha.

Ryan turned to Martha and put his arm around her as she gave him a welcoming hug. "Well, you're in luck," he said. "I'm gonna cook the best pizza, *ever*, tonight."

Keri said, "I went ahead and prepared the dough, so everything is ready. All you have to do is roll it out, put the toppings on, and toss it in the oven."

"Fantastic! That'll save us a couple of hours."

"So, what happened at work today?"

"It can wait. Let me get cleaned up and we can put the pizzas in the oven."

If I get into it now, I won't have her full attention.

David stepped into the room and waved at his dad. Ryan waved back and signed, "You okay?"

"Fine," David signed.

"Me clean up," Ryan signed. "Then cook pizza."

"Okay," David signed.

While he changed into jeans and a T-shirt, Ryan's mind whirled. Until he told Keri every detail concerning his discussion with John Dross, his world would be out of balance. Regardless of what she thought, he intended to call John and arrange an informational meeting. His three biggest concerns were the salary, the job location, and travel time away from home. As a minimum, the pay must exceed his current salary and hopefully enough to allow Keri to stop working. There was a slim chance Keri would be interested in moving and a no-brainer that she would not be too happy about him being away from home all week.

✈ ✈ ✈

As the credits rolled, a surge of adrenaline rushed through his veins. Finally he and Keri could talk.

The children left for their rooms and Keri began straightening the pillows, arranging them neatly on the sofa. Ryan said, "I'm dying to tell you what happened at work."

"Oh, that's right," Keri said.

"Can you sit down while we talk? This is important."

"Sure, I'd love to." Keri sat beside him and kissed him on the cheek. Her playful attitude made him smile. He needed her balance to soften his overly-serious side, always thinking too hard about the details. He blamed it on his profession as a pilot, constantly analyzing the worst-case scenarios before they occurred.

"One of my students today offered me a job."

Keri sat up. "What kind of job?"

"He is the chief pilot for a company based in Atlanta. It sounds like an amazing organization."

"Ryan, are you sure you want to do that again? I thought we decided to put an end to the traveling once we move to Georgia. I had hoped our lives were going to be different."

"I know, but just think...it might pay enough for you to stop working and stay at home with the kids...even allow us to pay off our debts more quickly. I just can't help thinking that this job might be the answer to a lot of our problems."

"So what's the job like? I mean...what does it pay? How long would you be away from home on trips?"

"Well...I don't know about the pay and travel yet."

"Ryan, I hate to see you get your hopes up until you at least have a little more information."

"The chief pilot, John Dross, seemed eager for me to call him and set up a meeting."

"That sounds good. Why don't you do that first?"

Ryan could tell that Keri had little interest in learning more about a job that would require him to be on the road...even in the best of circumstances. In addition, after what they had been through, she had made it clear she was not too excited about him flying at all. "I'll give him a call tomorrow morning and set something up. He said he would be out of town next week, so it will be a few days before we can meet."

John reminded his copilot about a trip to San Juan in the morning. The copilot said he would be at the hangar by six. I'll call John at six-thirty.

Keri stood and took Ryan's hand. "What do you say about calling it an early evening and do some reading in bed...or whatever?" She pulled him to his feet and kissed him.

"Sounds good."

CHAPTER 4

Buckhead, Georgia
Saturday morning—August 2004

*R*yan woke at 5:45 a.m. eager to call John Dross. He eased out of bed, slipped on a pair of jeans and a Polo shirt, then headed downstairs and out the garage door.

After a short five minute drive, he wheeled into the neighborhood shopping center and parked in front of Starbucks. He checked the time: 6:12.

Sitting in his car, he pulled John's business card from his pocket and dialed the number.

On the second ring John answered. "Hello."

"John, this is Ryan Mitchell."

"Hi, Ryan, I'm glad you called."

"I remembered you had a trip this morning and I wanted to call before you left. Any chance we could set up a meeting next week?"

"Absolutely! We're off to San Juan for a couple of days, but if nothing unexpected happens, I'll be back home Monday afternoon. I would love to meet with you on Tuesday if that works for you."

"Sounds good. I have a simulator early Tuesday

morning, but I'm free after eleven o'clock."

"How about lunch on Tuesday."

"Great."

"I'll call you Monday night and we can decide on a place to meet."

After hanging up, Ryan gazed at John's business card. He imagined the best case scenario: A salary large enough to allow Keri to stop working; minimal time away from home; based in Atlanta.

God, could this be from you?

He held the door for a woman exiting the coffee shop while she balanced her tray of four coffees.

"Thank you," the woman said.

"You're welcome." Ryan caught the wafting aroma of the fresh brew and drew it in. "Looks like someone will be excited to see you."

"I have relatives visiting from Alabama."

"Well...have a great day and enjoy your family...and the coffee."

"Thank you," she said.

As Ryan turned, he drew in a different scent lingering in the wake of the woman's path. He inhaled deeply. The sweet fragrance was apparently the woman's perfume.

Nice.

After only a few steps into the coffee shop, the rich flavor of brewed coffee and freshly ground beans quickly replaced the lingering scent of perfume.

Ryan approached the cashier, but before he gave his order, he turned his head. "Ahhh...choo!"

"God bless you," the barista said.

"Thank you."

"What can I get you?"

"I'll have a Grande drip, no room, please."

Ryan paid the cashier then took his coffee to the condiment bar and added a sweetener and some milk. As he headed toward the door, he shielded his nose. "Ahhh...choo!"

Man, something must be in the air.

Seated in his car, he placed his coffee in the cupholder between the seats. "Ah...choo!" He wiped his nose with a napkin, then rubbed his itchy eyes.

What is going on?

He took a careful sip of the hot coffee which helped clear his sinuses. He sneezed again.

Could it be the coffee?

By the time he had driven the short distance to his condo, the sneezing had grown into a full-blown allergic reaction—burning, itchy, and teary eyes accompanied by random, uncontrollable sneezing.

If something in the environment had caused his outbreak, it should have affected him earlier. He quickly dismissed the idea of a coffee allergy.

The woman's perfume! It must be an allergic reaction to her perfume.

He pulled into the garage and hurried inside. Keri was sitting at the kitchen table drinking coffee and reading her Bible.

"Ahhhh...choo!"

"God bless you," she said.

He rubbed his burning eyes. "Ahh...choo!"

"My goodness! I hope you're not getting sick?" She looked at his face. "Your eyes..."

"No. I think it's an allergic reaction. I'll be fine. I need to lie down for a minute." From experience with occasional allergies, his only relief—other than drugs—was to wash his face, lie down, close his eyes, and let the allergens settle and the histamines calm down.

"Let me know if I can do anything for you."

"I'm good. I just need to lie down and be still."

After washing his face and blowing his nose, he headed

for the bedroom where he laid flat on his back on the bed and closed his eyes. Within minutes he found relief.

I'll be fine once I give my system a chance to settle down.

He drifted off to sleep…

Ryan exchanged money with a street-side vendor for one of his bagels. The cloudless morning sky gave way to the warmth of the sun as the shadows from towering skyscrapers slowly dissolved.

I'm dreaming. I'm in New York…on a layover.

"Ryan?" A woman's voice called his name causing him to turn. "Is that you?"

"Keri!" How are you doing?" He gave her an innocent hug.

Keri is here with me.

"Great! How about you?" She stepped back.

"Doing good," he said. "What a coincidence to be on a layover in New York on the same day."

"Yeah, amazing. So, how's Emily?"

That's right…I was married to Emily then.

He paused, searching for the right words. "She's good."

No, she's not! Tell her the truth!

"You still enjoying California?" he said.

"Yeah. I especially *love* the weather…and there's so much to do," she said. "How is Emily adjusting to Texas?"

He folded the paper bag around his bagel. "She wasn't too fond of it at first, but I think she's slowly accepting it."

Stop lying! Emily hates it!

"I can understand why she might have issues with Texas, especially the heat."

He stepped aside to let a man place an order with the street vendor. "I planned on walking to Central Park. I'd love for you to join me. It would give us a chance to catch up on things. I need to tell you the latest about Mom."

"Is she okay?"

"She's fine, but it looks like there are some challenges ahead for us all."

"I was headed to the park, myself. I really do want to hear about Martha." They started walking slowly toward the park.

They stopped briefly on the corner of 7th and Central Park South (59th Street) waiting for the traffic light to change. They walked across the street and along the sidewalk leading into the park.

As if they entered another world, the cool air beneath the canopy of trees and grassy lawns invited them to relax. Rollerbladers, joggers, and bikers glided by on the smooth asphalt. The clip-clop of horse's hooves pulling carriages replaced blaring horns and screeching tires. The sounds of the city grew muffled and less noticeable the farther they walked into the park. A refuge from the chaotic city life: 843 acres stretching from 59th Street to 110th Street.

As they walked, he continued to talk about his mother. "You won't believe what she said."

"What?"

"While I visited with her, she wanted to know if you and I ever flew together at the airline."

"That's understandable; after all, she knows I'm a flight attendant."

"But that's not what she meant. She thinks you are Emily."

Keri's eyes widened. "You mean she thinks..." she trailed off.

Ryan nodded. "Yep. She thinks I married you, rather than Emily. Or she thinks Emily is you...or...well, you know what I mean."

Go ahead! Tell her how you wish things had turned out

*like mom thought they should have. Tell her that you wish
you had married her.*

"How do you know for sure that's what she meant?"

"She specifically asked me if, *Keri*, liked living in
Texas…with me." He turned to her and smiled.

While he dreamed, pleasant sensations charged through
his body and thoughts. Memories of that day were fresh and
exhilarating. Outside of his dream, he knew he was married
to Keri, but inside the dream, he was lucid and aware of his
dream character's every feeling.

"You hungry?" Ryan asked.

"I guess I could eat something."

"Let me buy you lunch." He held out the bag he'd been
carrying since they met in front of the hotel. "I'll share."

"I've got a better idea," she said. "I know where there's
a great little deli over between Madison and Park Avenues.
That is…if you don't mind walking a couple of blocks."

"Sounds great." He lifted his bag once more. "And if we
get lost, we've always got my bagel." They laughed.

"The place is called Delmonico Gourmet Food Market.
They've got just about everything from salads to gourmet
specialty sandwiches, and the prices are very reasonable."
She checked her watch. "It's just a little after eleven, so we
should beat most of the lunch crowd."

"So, how far is this place?" Ryan asked, jokingly.

She reached over and playfully squeezed him on his
side. It was a habit from the past; something she'd done
many times before. "The walk will do you good."

"I should have seen that coming." He chuckled.
"Hopefully, I won't pass out."

They crossed Madison Avenue beneath the shadows of
towering buildings, the cool winds swirled through the
streets. The smell of fresh bread and pizza filled the air.

"Here it is," she said.

He reached for the door, holding it open while she

entered, following her close behind.

Ryan ordered the grilled chicken breast sandwich from the SPECIALTY SANDWICHES menu. It came with roasted peppers, basil oil, and red lettuce on crusty ciabatta bread. He also added a bowl of Manhattan clam chowder. Keri ordered from the CREATE YOUR OWN SALAD menu: a grilled chicken and asparagus salad with mandarin oranges and roasted peppers topped with a mandarin vinaigrette dressing.

After settling with the cashier, Ryan looked around for a place to sit. Not liking what he saw, he said, "How about we head back to the park for a picnic?"

"I've got a better idea."

"What could be better than a picnic in Central Park?"

She is about to ask you to go to her dad's condo. Don't do it!

"I was just thinking…we could grab a cab and head over to my dad's condo. It's not far from here, and I know you've always wanted to see it."

"Does he mind?"

Don't let her talk you into it. I know you want to get her alone, but it turns out bad. Don't do it!

"Not at all, he even gave me a key," she said. "He hardly ever uses the place, except for business. Most of the time it just sits empty."

The area from 59th street to 96th street, between Central Park and the East River was noted for having some of the most luxurious and expensive residences in the world. It was a place where New York's rich are shrouded behind thick walls, guarded by uniformed-doormen with ermine collars; where children go to elite private schools, and the subway stations even seem cleaner.

As chronicled by Tom Wolfe in his novel, *Bonfire of the Vanities*, it is an area touting a "who's who" list of retail stores, art galleries, museums, restaurants, and expensive boutiques: Tiffany, Louis Vuitton, Chanel, Gucci, Christie's, Sotheby's, the Guggenheim, and FAO Schwartz. Some said it even surpassed the Ginza in Tokyo as the most expensive retail area in the world.

I've been here. I know how this plays out. You won't be able to control yourself. It was a terrible mistake! It is wrong! You MUST make a different choice...even if it is only a dream.

Ryan's dream double looked at her. "Keri, as much as I would love to see your dad's place, it would probably not be a good idea for us to go there alone."

You're doing the right thing!

"You're probably right."

Now...quick...before you change your mind, grab a cab to the park.

"It's a beautiful day. Let's grab a cab back to the park," his dream double said.

"Sounds good."

✈ ✈ ✈

Keri was sitting on the edge of the bed when Ryan opened his eyes. "It's time to wake up, sleepyhead," she said.

"How long did I sleep?"

"About eight hours."

"Eight hours? Are you sure?"

How could that be? I was just taking a nap!

"Let's just say you've slept long enough."

She must be messing with me.

He cleared his thoughts, thankful he was married to such a wonderful woman. He stared into her brown eyes. "I'm blessed we ended up together." He took her hand and rubbed it.

She smiled, leaned down, and kissed him gently. "We were meant to be together from the beginning."

"You won't believe what I dreamed," he said.

"What?"

"Do you remember that day in New York when we met on our layovers? I was married to Emily and you were about to be married to Rex...which, by the way, I didn't know anything about at the time."

"How could I forget?"

"Well, in my dream, the entire day was replayed with one exception; we never went to your dad's condo."

"What do you mean?"

Not sure why she was confused, he clarified, "In my dream, after we got our lunch at the deli, we went back to Central Park *instead* of going to your dad's condo."

With a puzzled look, Keri said, "I don't understand what you are talking about. What gave you the idea we went to my dad's condo? Is that something you dreamed?"

"Keri, are you messing with me? You know what we did."

Keri said, "I remember we bumped into each other in front of the hotel where you were staying. You were getting a bagel. We walked to Central Park and you told me about your mom. Remember? Then we walked to Delmonico's Food Market, picked up lunch, and took a cab back to the park where we had a picnic. How could you forget?"

"Why are you saying this? You know we went to your dad's condo, right?"

"Ryan, we never went to my dad's condo that day! I think I would remember that. However, I do remember mentioning to you that I normally went there on layovers, but when I brought it up, you said it wouldn't be a good idea to go there alone. I agreed. So instead, we went to the park and had a wonderful picnic."

"Keri! Why are you messing with me?"

Keri turned her head toward the bedroom door at the sound of Martha's voice. "Mom, I'm hungry."

"I'm coming," Keri said.

"Keri, you can't go! Either I'm losing my mind or you are really testing my patience with your little game."

"How much longer," Martha said.

"Just a minute, darling."

"Martha," Ryan said, "let David fix your lunch. Mom and I need to talk."

"Dad you are silly," Martha said, as she headed for the kitchen.

"My wife thinks I'm crazy and now my daughter calls me silly."

Keri turned to Ryan. In a stern voice she said, "Your five-year-old daughter thinks you are silly because you suggested her little brother should fix her breakfast...and I don't think you are crazy...just forgetful."

"Wait! What did you say?"

"I said you are not crazy..."

"No. What do you mean her 'little' brother? David is fifteen."

"Ryan? Are you okay?" Keri paused. "Oh, I get it. So now you want to mess with *me*?"

"What are you talking about?"

"Ryan, what is wrong with you? You know we just celebrated David's second birthday last week."

"Keri, you're taking this too far." Ryan got out of bed. The room spun like a slow moving carousel.

I must have stood up too fast. I need to find David.

"Where are you going?" she asked, following close behind.

"To find David and stop this ridiculous game." Ryan hurried down the hallway to David's bedroom. On the floor in the middle of the room sat a two-year-old boy playing with a model airplane. Ryan turned to Keri and asked, "Who is that boy?"

"Are you serious?"

"Keri, please don't joke with me. Where is David?"

"Ryan, he's right in front of you! That little boy is your son."

CHAPTER 5

Buckhead, Georgia
Saturday morning—August 2004

Standing in the doorway, staring at the two-year-old boy, Ryan said, "That's impossible!" He laughed out loud. "Somebody pleeease tell me what's going on?"

Keri put her arm around him and led him back into the bedroom. "Honey, why don't you lie down."

Slightly dizzy and spatially disoriented, Ryan followed Keri willfully to the bedroom and did as she requested. "How can this be happening?"

"Ryan, I don't know why you're so confused."

"I'm not confused!" He rose up on the bed.

"Calm down...everything is going to be alright." She eased him back down. "We just need to talk this out." Keri sat quietly for a few seconds rubbing his hand. "That must have been one doozy of a dream."

"I feel like I'm living parallel lives. Part of me knows that little boy is my son, but another part of me believes just as strongly our son, David, should be fifteen years old." He sat up quickly. "I didn't notice! Is our son deaf?"

"No! What makes you think that?"

"I don't know. I just remember—or dreamed...I'm not sure which—that our son is...was...deaf."

It seems so real that we had a fifteen-year-old deaf son named David. Why?

"Well, you definitely dreamed it."

"Keri, it's hard to explain...I don't even know if I understand what's going on. All I know is that in my dream, I knew if we went to the condo, we would be overcome with passion for each other, and would regret it for the rest of our lives. It was as if it had already happened in some *other* life."

"Regret what?"

"That you would get pregnant with David. That is why I believed we had a fifteen-year-old son...we were in New York fifteen years ago. The timing would have been perfect."

"That would have been a mess."

"No joke."

"Well, I'm proud of you." She patted his hand. "You could have done anything without consequences, but you did the right thing. That shows you are a man of character, even when you are dreaming."

"If you say so," he said, still confused.

It did make sense that if they didn't go to the condo, Keri would not have gotten pregnant. Therefore, the fifteen-year-old version of David would have never been born. He began to settle into the idea that his *other* life, regardless of how real it seemed to him, was nothing more than a dream within a dream.

"So other than the rendezvous at the condo," Keri said, "is there anything else you dreamed we did, or didn't do, I should know about?"

He laughed. "No, everything in the dream I believed to have happened after that day in New York, has happened. Emily left me. You married Rex. You caught him cheating and y'all divorced. Then we got married and lived happily ever after. That is the way it goes, doesn't it?"

Keri leaned over and kissed him. "Yes. And the frog turned into a prince." They both laughed. "Let's hope you don't have any more nightmares like that."

He said, "Do you think the perfume had anything to do with my crazy dream?"

"What perfume?"

"The perfume that gave me the allergic reaction."

"You didn't say anything about any perfume in your dream. Plus, I don't think you can smell inside your dreams."

Why doesn't she remember the allergic reaction?

"Don't you remember? When I came back from Starbucks I was sneezing. I went to the bedroom and took a nap."

"Maybe in your dream. You just slept late, and I woke you up so you wouldn't miss our traditional Saturday morning breakfast."

That's strange. She really doesn't remember. Maybe I'm still confused.

"Well…maybe it *was* in my dream, but what if there *was* an imaginary perfume that did have magical powers that would allow a person to travel back in time and change things in their past?"

"Okay…so just for fun, let's assume you jump in your time machine and gas it up with perfume. Where would be your first stop?"

"That's a no-brainer. First, I would travel back to a time before I ever met Emily Anderson, and I would have never married her. Then I would find you and marry you before Rex had a chance to meet you. From there, I would search for every mistake I had ever made and fix them all."

"That sounds nice." She kissed him again. "While you work on fixing our past, I'll fix us breakfast."

From her playful banter, he could tell she had no recollection of his allergic attack. "Sounds good. I'll take a quick shower."

"You have fifteen minutes," she said.

"No problem. Oh, Keri, I forgot to tell you... I called John this morning and set up a meeting with him for Tuesday at lunch."

"Good. It will be interesting to learn more about the job."

While showering, he searched for details of any memory of some *other* life—imagined or dreamed. Every detail in his dream was vivid and clear. His memory of the events that occurred at the condo in New York was as real as the skin on his body. The concerns he had as a father raising a deaf child could not have been imagined. As hard as he tried, it was impossible to accept that it was simply a dream within a dream. But could he have actually lived another life?

That's preposterous.

Then how could he explain being completely awake, staring at his own two-year-old son, and not recognizing him? Was he sleepwalking?

The events that occurred in his imagined *other* life were too real to dismiss, but too crazy to believe. And the freakish possibility he had somehow altered his present reality from within his dream was even more ridiculous. It had been almost an hour and the details of his dream had not faded as they so often do. He could easily sit down and write out verbatim, as a novelist might tell a story—every event, every emotion, and practically every word spoken in his *other* life. How would that be possible if what he had imagined was only a dream within a dream? Did he have some special gift?

Hardly.

If *Keri* had no recollection of another life, *no one* would believe him.

Is it possible the perfume had some twisted affect on my mind? Could it happen again? It couldn't hurt to try.

To conduct the experiment, he needed the exact fragrance, but there was no way he could describe it. He could sample fragrances all day at a cosmetic department, but if he sampled more than one fragrance, it would be impossible to isolate which fragrance caused the reaction.

He needed to find the woman who was wearing the perfume, but he had no clue who she was or where she lived. Her relatives were visiting from Alabama and she was taking them their morning coffee. She must live in Buckhead...near that particular Starbucks. More than likely, she is a regular customer. There's a chance she will return in the morning wanting to continue her hospitality for her visiting relatives.

He would be waiting.

CHAPTER 6

Buckhead, Georgia
Saturday morning—August 2004

Keri had the kitchen smelling like an IHOP Restaurant—homemade buttermilk biscuits in the oven, pancakes, scrambled eggs, grits on the stove, and bacon sizzling in the microwave. A "big breakfast"—as she called it—was a Saturday morning tradition at the Mitchell house.

Martha and David waited patiently at the table for the first delivery of pancakes. "Here they come," Keri said, as she shoveled up two fluffy pancakes and transferred them to the kid's plates like a seasoned short-order cook. "More where those came from when you're finished," she said. "Martha, would you please cut up David's pancake and help him with the syrup?"

"Okaay," Martha said, sounding like it was a burden to help her little brother, but Keri knew she loved mothering him.

On the outside, Keri gave the impression it was a typical, carefree Saturday morning, while her interior world wobbled on its axis, unbalanced and uncertain. Something wasn't just right with Ryan. How could anyone explain the way he acted? She couldn't believe hearing his words 'Who is that boy?' as he stood looking at his son; then to persist they had lived some *other* life she knew nothing about.

Could it be dementia, or even worse, the onset of Alzheimer's? He's too young for that.

Researchers did not know the exact cause of the disease, but they did know it is most likely due to a combination of a variety of genetic factors. Ryan's mom had Alzheimer's which compelled Keri to be circumspect that Ryan might be at risk in his later years...but not this early.

"Thank the Lord for Saturday mornings," Ryan said. He gave Keri a kiss as she passed in front of him on her way to scoop up more pancakes.

From now on she would listen watchfully to every word, always hoping nothing he said would reinforce her concerns of dementia. The thought of her losing him mentally at such a young age, and having to care for her young children alone, was unbearable.

"So who's up for a field trip today?" Keri said.

"What did you have in mind," Ryan said.

"I thought it would be nice to take a drive...maybe show the kids where we grew up. We've been here over a year and haven't explored our old stomping ground yet. Let's pretend we're on a treasure hunt."

"That'll be fun mom," Martha said.

The treasure hunt Keri was thinking of was not in the visible world around them, but instead, along the neural pathways of Ryan's brain. Exposing him to his past might trigger the presence of damaged neurotransmitters responsible for disrupting the cell-to-cell transfer of electrical currents over synapses connecting neurons. She needed to confirm any confusion or loss of memory as soon as possible. Dementia and Alzheimer's is a sneaky disease, often creeping into the mind of its victim as much as twenty years before a diagnosis can be made—long before family members recognize it. The earlier it is detected, the earlier treatment can commence.

"That sounds like a great idea," Ryan said. "It's definitely a beautiful day for a drive."

This is exactly what Ryan needed—visiting their old high school, seeing Keri's old family home where she grew up, and the overall feel and sense of a time when his thoughts were in a different place—not yet scarred by the consequences of unwise decisions.

He planned to drive into Keri's driveway and sit in the exact spot where she had driven the dagger of separation into his heart. He wanted to remember every emotion and retrace every step.

Looking back, that one event on Saturday, June 23, 1974, was the catalyst that eventually destroyed all hope of the perfect life they had dreamed about—thanks to Barbara Ann Hart. It was only by God's grace he and Keri found each other in the end, but the thought of "what could have been" festered in his mind.

His mother had warned him to be on guard for the deceptiveness hidden within the human heart, but his youthful ebullience blinded him from her wisdom. Instead, he defaulted to be schooled by life's merciless teacher.

He wished he could live it over again, but this time with his current knowledge of the consequences that had transpired.

Wouldn't it be great if a person could go back in time and alter past mistakes simply by the whiff of a sweet perfume? Each ounce would be priceless.

CHAPTER 7

Buckhead, Georgia
Saturday morning—August 2004

*S*tately homes and jaw-dropping grounds and gardens *make* Buckhead the Beverly Hills of Atlanta, the magazine article stated—the South at its best with Southern mansions spread atop rolling, green lawns sprinkled with magnolias, pink and white dogwoods, and beds of flowering azaleas.

Ryan cruised the quiet, tree-lined streets of Buckhead, while his thoughts and emotions explored his distant past, often sparked by the slightest remembrances—a curve in the road, an old oak tree, a particular house.

Turning off West Paces Ferry onto Habersham Road, a place he had driven thousands of times before on his way to and from Keri's house, he experienced an out-of-body sensation. "Surreal, isn't it?" he said.

"As though it was only yesterday," Keri said, "and it all looks exactly the same."

After making a quick visit to Pace Academy on West Paces Ferry where Keri and Ryan first met, Ryan was eager to see Keri's old house.

"I would love to meet the people who bought the house after the bank repossessed it from us," he said.

"It would only make me sad, knowing we should be the ones living there."

He slowed before pulling into the driveway. "Well, the gate is open, so I'm considering that an invitation."

"Ryan, are you sure this is a good idea?"

"I just want to sit in the driveway for five minutes. If someone comes out of the house, I'll tell them this was your old family home and we just wanted to take a peek. All I need is five minutes."

He turned into the driveway and through the opened wrought-iron gate. The winding drive cut across an immaculately manicured lawn beneath towering oaks and to the front of a large, Georgian-style home. He stopped the car as close to the exact position he remembered to be the spot where he had parked on that Saturday night long ago. "This is it…the exact spot where you dumped me."

"Yep," Keri said. "Can we, please, go now?"

"I'll never forget the shock when you said 'I think we need to break up'. It totally caught me off guard."

The house was quiet. So far, the owners were unaware that strangers had driven into their driveway. Ryan imagined a maid hard at work inside polishing silver, the lady of the house out shopping for more clothes to stuff into one of her many closets, and the breadwinner flipping deals worth hundreds of thousands over a weekend game of golf.

Keri said, "I was young and stupid. I remember running inside and meeting my mother at the door, waiting for me like a prison guard. I screamed at her, pushed her aside, and ran to my room and cried. I was so confused and my heart ached like never before. Even after having broken up with you, I still felt connected to you. After you left for the Naval Academy, I was determined to write you every day. However, it didn't take long before my letters went unanswered. I assumed I'd lost you."

"I was a fool. A stupid fool. I should've kept writing. I should have visited you on my breaks from school. The longer we were apart, the less it seemed possible we would ever be together again. Keri, if I had it to do over again, it would be different."

"How?"

"I would have never let you leave my car that night. Maybe I would have kidnapped you. I don't know what I would have done...probably something crazy."

"Mommy, I'm tired of sitting here. Can we go now?" Martha said.

"Ryan, I think we better go." Keri faced Martha with a big smile. "I think it's time for that ice cream we talked about, don't you?"

"Yipeee! Ice cream!" Martha turned to David in his carseat and said, "Can you say cookie?"

"Cookie...cookie...cookie," David said. On special outings to get ice cream, David always preferred a cookie. It was a special cookie in the shape of a windmill.

"Ryan," Keri said, "look in the rearview mirror."

"Why, are we in trouble?"

She reached up and adjusted the mirror so he could see Martha and David in the backseat. "We might have made some mistakes along the way, but I think we have a lot to be thankful for."

"That's for sure." Ryan smiled.

"I'm not so sure I would change anything. How could our lives have turned out any better?"

He didn't answer.

He drove the car around the circular drive and eased down the driveway and back onto Habersham Road. He continued to cogitate on that Saturday night in 1974 when he left Keri's house.

He pulled to the curb.

"What's wrong?" Keri said.

"After I left your house that night, it was this exact spot where I remembered the note you slipped into my front pocket. This is where I pulled to the curb and read it.

"Dated June 23, 1974, it read: *I believe if we are meant to be, nothing can keep us apart. As long as I live, I will patiently wait on each sunrise and follow each sunset into tomorrow, for I believe it is the path of the sun that will lead us to our hopes and dreams. Promise me that you will never lose hope in tomorrow. I love you, Keri.*"

"Wow! I'm impressed."

"I reread that note hundreds of times...if not thousands, eventually memorizing it. I never understood how you could write such a note, knowing you were about to dump me."

"You missed one thing when you read the note that night," she said.

"What?"

"The tears that had dripped onto the paper while I wrote." With compassion in her eyes, she said, "Ryan, I am so sorry for the pain I caused you that night. It shouldn't have ended like that."

"If only I could go back and live that night over again...just that one night."

"The first sentence in my note held true: *if we are meant to be, nothing can keep us apart*. We were definitely meant to be...and we are together. What more could we ask for?"

"I guess you're right. Who needs a time machine when we have everything we could have ever hoped for?"

"I've never told you, but I must give your mother most of the credit for the note."

"My mother?"

"I'm sure you remember the needlepoint she gave us on our wedding day...the one that hangs in the foyer by our front door."

"Yeah. I even remember watching her make it."

"The words on the needlepoint were her mission statement in life: *I will continue to patiently wait on each sunrise and follow each sunset into tomorrow for I believe it is the path of the sun that will lead us to our hopes and dreams.*"

"She was an amazing woman," he said. "I miss her."

"After you left for the Academy, I spent many hours that summer being counseled by your mother. I can hear her saying, 'The rest of your life begins right now. You need to forget the past, embrace the present, and put your hope in the future.' Ryan, we can't change the past…all we have is the present and the future. Your mother would have never approved of a time machine. Her focus was always on the present."

"I wish I had not been so butt-headed and had paid more attention to mom's advice. Maybe if I had, I wouldn't need a time machine. I even remember her warning me about girls like Emily Anderson."

Keri chuckled. "Did she warn you about me?"

"She loved you. She always believed we would eventually get together. I'm sure she's looking down from Heaven now with a smile on her face."

"I'm sure she is."

"Mommy…"

"Okay, darling. We're going."

Ryan continued down Habersham Road to Wesley Road and then north on Peachtree toward the ice cream shop—the one that sold David's favorite windmill cookies.

The idea of a time machine might sound a bit far-fetched, but he was determined to give the sweet smelling fragrance one more chance. But first he had to find the woman named Angel.

CHAPTER 8

Buckhead, Georgia
Sunday morning—August 2004

*R*yan woke early, quietly dressed, slipped out of the house, and arrived at Starbucks at 5:30 a.m.

He parked in the same spot as the previous morning. Having just opened, the coffee shop was quiet, but it wouldn't be long before caffeine-starved customers filed into the store eager for their morning shot of Java.

Ryan ordered a Tall coffee and sat in the corner near the window where he could observe the parking lot. Recognizing the woman shouldn't be a problem. When she arrived, he would allow her time to place her order and then wait until she stopped at the condiment bar before approaching her.

By six o'clock a steady flow of customers were drifting into the store. At 6:15 a.m., he saw her. He watched as she made her way to the counter and ordered four coffees—two Talls and two Grandes. She paid for the coffees and headed for the condiment bar. He stood and moved in close behind her—not too close—just close enough to take in a deep whiff of the familiar, sweet fragrance of her perfume.

Ahhhh...that's it.

He moved to her right, now standing shoulder-to-shoulder at the condiment bar. Pretending to have just purchased his coffee, he took a stir stick and swirled it in his half-filled cup of coffee. He drew in another slow, quiet breath, encouraging the fragrance to consume him. "So I see your relatives are still in town," he said, hoping to delay her.

She looked up at him, pausing briefly before saying, "Oh, yes. You held the door for me yesterday morning. How could I forget?"

Ryan felt a sneeze building, ready to explode. He quickly turned his head away from the woman. "Ahhh...chooo!"

"God bless you," she said.

"Thank you." He had to act quickly before being overcome by the impending allergy and melting into a drippy mess. He needed the name of the perfume in case he never saw the woman again.

Fighting to hold back another sneeze, he said, "I wondered if you might tell me the name of the perfume you're wearing today. I think my wife would love it."

"It's called *Angel*...been around for at least ten years. I've been wearing it since it first came out. Having my name on the bottle makes it special."

"That's very interesting. If you don't mind me asking, where did you buy the perfume?"

"Are you from around here?"

"Yes. I live in Buckhead."

"I purchased mine at Macy's in the Lenox Square Mall. They have a large display on their front counter. You can't miss it."

"Thanks." He turned his head away from Angel. "Ahhh...chooo!"

"God bless you."

"Thank you...again."

"I hope it is not my perfume causing you to sneeze. If so,

you might want to rethink your gift for your wife."

"No...it's probably something else. Thank you, Angel. I'll be sure to pick some up. I love the fragrance." His eyes were starting to burn and itch. He covered his nose. "Ahh...choo!"

"God bless you," Angel said.

"All I need is some fresh air," he lied. Ryan held the door for Angel as she managed her tray of coffees. "Have a wonderful day."

She placed her tray of coffees on the roof of a large four-door Mercedes-Benz sedan. He questioned whether he should offer to help. "Ahhh...chooo!" Maybe not.

She opened the door, retrieved the coffees from the roof, and leaned in and placed the coffee carrier on the floor in front of the passenger's seat.

She must be relatively wealthy.

As she backed the Benz out of the parking spot, he noticed a Georgia license plate with the peach in the center and MORGAN County on the bottom.

"Ahh...choo!" The allergens were fast at work racing through his bloodstream preparing him for what he hoped would be another time-traveling dream into the past. If not, he could safely assume that the mystery of his *other* life was without a doubt only a dream within a dream. However, if miraculously the sweet smelling potion spun him into another life, he could easily purchase more *Angel* perfume.

When he arrived home, Keri was sitting at the kitchen table sipping coffee and reading her Bible.

"Ahhhh...choo!"

"God bless you," she said.

He rubbed his burning eyes. "Ahh...choo!"

"My goodness! I hope you're not getting sick?" She looked at his face. "Your eyes..."

Déjà vu. That is exactly what she said yesterday morning.

"No. I think it's an allergic reaction. I'll be fine. I need to lie down for a minute."

"Can I do anything for you?"

"No. I'm going to lie down and let this stuff wear off. I should be okay in time to go to church. Just give me an hour or so to sleep it off."

Ryan wasted no time washing his face, blowing his nose, and getting in bed. He had purposely stayed up late the previous night hoping to enhance his sleep quality—assuming he would find the woman and ingest the perfume.

Within ten minutes he began feeling groggy.

The condo was empty. He glanced at his watch—four-thirty, seven-thirty Atlanta time. His mom would be expecting his call. He always called her on her birthday regardless of where he was in the world. He imagined her sitting in her favorite chair, working her needle like a skilled surgeon, bringing a drab piece of canvas to life with one of her heart-felt scenes—each with its own special meaning about life.

He grabbed a bottle of water from the fridge, took a seat on the sofa in the den, and dialed her number.

"Hello?" she said.

"Happy birthday, Mom!"

"Ryan, so happy to hear your voice! How are you doing?"

"Good. Did you have a good day?"

"Well, at my age, they're all good." She chuckled.

Ryan pulled the phone over by the sofa, leaned back, and propped his feet up.

I'm dreaming. This is not real. It's happening again. I can change my life.

The lucidity of his dream was exceptionally brilliant. He had not only lived this experience in his past life, he was living it now.

This is awesome!

He could ask his mother anything. She would obviously not be aware of his current reality outside of his dream, because she had not lived it, but she would be fully aware of the imaginary reality within the dream.

She said, "Guess who I got a birthday card from yesterday?"

"Who?"

"Keri. She always remembers my birthday."

"Keri Hart?" Ryan sat up. "What did she say?"

"Not much. Just that she loved me, missed me, and wished me a happy birthday. She's so sweet."

"Where is she now?"

"She's in Florida... Ft. Lauderdale. Did I tell you she's a flight attendant?"

"Yeah. You mentioned it in one of your letters."

"I wish you two could get together."

"She is an amazing woman, isn't she?"

"Yes, she is. The two of you would be so perfect together."

"Mom, I miss you."

"I miss you, too. When are you going to come visit me?

"Soon...very soon."

"Well, you better not dilly dally or you are going to lose that sweet little thing."

"Does she ever ask about me?"

"I keep her up to speed with what is going on in your crazy life. We don't see each other much anymore. Just a few letters every now and then. Do you remember that night before you left for the Academy?"

"How could I forget? She dumped me cold...but I know her mother was the mastermind behind it."

"I never told you, but the next day, she came over and we had a long heart-to-heart talk. I'd never seen her so sad.

She was a mess. And you were right; Barbara Ann *did* encourage her to break up with you."

"I knew it!"

"Keri hated herself, but felt trapped. The poor little thing was so befuddled. I hated seeing her suffer. She loved you more than life itself. She said she would do anything to take back that night. I told her not to give up, that you would understand. She decided to write you every day. But you know, it takes two to keep a relationship alive and you weren't exactly the best at writing."

"You don't have to rub it in, but in my defense, they were busting my chops. I barely had time to brush my teeth."

"Ryan, you could have…"

"Okay Mom, I know. I blew it…should've written her more…I screwed up. But I'm going to fix all that now."

"Why don't you write her now? She knows you're in California. I think it would be nice. I know she would love to hear from you." A moment of silence followed.

"I've got a better idea. Do you have her number?"

"No. We agreed not to call, only write, because I really can't afford long distance, and I don't want her wasting her money. Let me give you her address."

He grabbed a notepad and a pen. "What is it?" He scribbled it down. "Mom, you were right about everything."

"What do you mean?"

Mom won't understand what I'm about to say, but I need to tell her.

"Mom, I should have listened to you and done what you said. I made a mess of my life. Things turned out okay, but I could have avoided a lot of pain and misery if I had only listened."

"Ryan, you are still young. You have all of your life ahead of you. Don't focus on the short past. Remember, learn from the past, embrace the present….

Ryan cut her off. "I know, I know…and hope in the

future. The needlepoint you made says it all."

"Yes it does, and it's hanging by the door so I'll always be reminded."

The needlepoint is actually hanging in our house, but she wouldn't know that because she had not given it to us yet.

"Mom, I love you."

"I love you, too. You sure are sentimental. Anything I need to know?"

"Just know that not a day goes by that I don't think of you, wish I could be with you, and talk to you more. My memory of you always brightens my day."

"You act like I've died. I'm still here...at least for now."

"It's hard to explain," he said. "But everything is fine...actually it is fantastic! Things are going to be different now."

They said good-bye.

He went to his bedroom and pulled out some paper and began writing:

Friday, May 13, 1983

Keri,

> *It's been a long time. I learned from Mom you're living in Florida. She tells me you're a flight attendant. Sounds exciting. I also hope to be hired by the airlines, once I complete my commitment to the Navy. Probably next summer.*

> *The Navy keeps me busy, and out of touch with everyone. Even Mom complains. I'm ready for a change. Maybe we can talk sometime and do some catching up. Mom didn't have your number. Mine is 619-231-1515. Please give me a call or write. I'm*

*living with a Navy buddy in Del Mar, a small
beach community north of San Diego.
I look forward to talking with you.*

*All my love,
Ryan*

This time, I'll hand-carry the letter to the mailbox.

As he licked the stamp, he heard the condo door close.
"What's up, buddy?" Rex called, as he made a beeline for the
fridge.

*Oh boy...the jerk is home to ruin my life. Well, not this
time.*

Ryan moved into the den. "Rex, did I ever tell you about
Keri Hart?"

*Why am I wasting my time telling Rex about Keri? I
know where this is going?*

Sprawled out on the sofa, half-way through his first beer,
Rex said. "Not sure."

"I haven't seen her since we split up back in high school,
but my mom tells me she is living in Florida and is a flight
attendant."

"Hey, dude, you'd better not go there. No telling what
she looks like now. She could be bald, bucktoothed, and the
size of a baby whale—a real swamp donkey."

"You're crazy! I know for a fact she is drop-dead
gorgeous."

"Not worth the chance. Too many babes out there for
you to waste your time thinking about some woman you
might not be able to recognize on a beach full of sea lions.
Yo, mate, let me grab my harpoon."

"Funny."

What a jerk. Why didn't I see this before?

"I'm going to contact her. If she'll have me, I'm going to
ask her to marry me," Ryan said.

"Man, what am I going to do with you? Really, dude, I think you're headed for the rocks."

"Rex, you have no clue."

"Remember, the Rexter tried to warn you." Rex picked up the TV remote, and started surfing. "Dude, you got a picture of this high-school hottie? Should I get my harpoon?"

"Not a current one."

"Hey, buddy, it's just one chick. Don't get bogged down over a memory when hundreds of gorgeous babes are out there waiting for us. I'm begging you to give them a chance." His tone lifted with enthusiasm. "Listen, let me take you to my favorite beach. It's a magical place. Dude, you won't *believe* the babes!" He smiled. "Your good buddy, Rex, is gonna take care of you. Trust me. Before the sun sets, you'll have forgotten all about Keri. She's no good for you. Dude, look at me." He stepped back and pointed at himself with both hands. "The Rexter knows."

Ryan stared at Rex.

It's a dream. It's happening again. If I go to that beach with Rex, I will meet Emily Anderson. That is where the trouble starts. If I stay home, I have a chance to change my entire future.

"Forget it, Rex! I'm sticking with what I know. You go without me this time."

"Dude! Have you lost your mind?"

"No. I think for once I'm going to make the right decision."

Once Ryan made his decision, Rex didn't seem to care. "Have it your way, dude."

Ryan retreated to his bedroom and stretched out on the bed. He remembered the note Keri stuffed in his pocket that night—their last night together.

He had kept it...but where? His Bible!

He sprung up, trying to remember where he might have put his Bible. He seldom read it, but his mother had given it to him when he was in high school. He kept it for sentimental reasons.

He rummaged through a box of books in his closet and found it. He fanned the thin pages releasing several pieces of paper to the floor. It only took a glance to spot the note, folded just as Keri had done before slipping it into his pocket that night. The sight of it flooded him with memories—good and bad.

June 23, 1974

Dear Ryan,

I believe if we are meant to be together, nothing can keep us apart. As long as I live, I will patiently wait on each sunrise and follow each sunset into tomorrow, for I believe it is the path of the sun that will lead us to our hopes and dreams. Promise me that you will never lose hope in tomorrow.

I love you,
Keri

He reread: *As long as I live, I will patiently wait on each sunrise and follow each sunset into tomorrow, for I believe it is the path of the sun that will lead us to our hopes and dreams...*

His mother's words echoed in his head, "Two souls that are meant to be together can never be separated."

✈ ✈ ✈

Ryan opened his eyes when Keri touched his arm. Not fully transitioned to reality, he looked around the room. It was confusingly different but somehow familiar at the same time.

"Wake up, sleepyhead, I don't want you to miss church," she said.

"How long did I sleep?"

"About eight hours."

"Did you say eight hours?"

"Maybe a little more."

That means she won't remember the allergic reaction—just like she didn't yesterday morning.

He tested her. "So, I slept all night and didn't wake up?"

"Like a dead man in a lumber yard—snoring away."

With his thoughts planted firmly in reality, he recalled his dream: He did not go to the beach with Rex, therefore, he did not meet Emily Anderson. He mailed his letter to Keri before Rex changed it. Shortly after she moved to California he married her—not Emily. Keri never married Rex.

CHAPTER 9

Southern California
Sunday Morning—April 2003

*R*yan's eyes widened with excitement. "Keri, it works! The perfume is magical!"

"Calm down. What perfume are you talking about?"

That's right...she won't remember anything that happened before I went to sleep—Starbucks; the perfume; the sneezing—none of it.

The choices he had made in his dream had changed everything. He was no longer in Georgia, but instead, back in California. It was as if they had never moved. It was April 2003.

He sat on the edge of the bed beside her.

She probably won't understand, but here goes...

"In my dream, I was in Rex's condo in Del Mar, back in 1983, when we were flight instructors at Miramar. I had just come home from work and I called my mom to wish her happy birthday. She started telling me about you and how you had sent her a birthday card. And then...I realized it was all a dream...a very clear, lucid dream. It was so weird!"

"It's not unusual to be lucid in your dreams. That has

been very thoroughly documented."

"But that's not all. I knew everything that had happened or was going to happen in that dream. It was like I had already lived it. My life was being replayed like a movie—a movie I had already seen. The only difference was I had the opportunity to make decisions that I knew were going to alter my future. For example, do you remember the letter you received from me while you were a flight attendant in Fort Lauderdale?"

"Of course I do. That letter was the reason we got back together and were eventually married. When I received that letter, I called you and we talked for two hours. I told you about my upcoming transfer to California in July and how excited I was about seeing you and reconnecting with you. You practically asked me to marry you on the phone. Just so you know, if you had asked me, I would have said yes. After that conversation, I knew we would be married soon."

She doesn't know. The only letter she received was the unaltered one...she is not aware that there ever was another letter.

Everything Keri said he knew to be true, but his mind struggled to understand his *other* life—the life he knew before he went to sleep.

Was it really only a dream?

In the midst of his dream it was impossible for him to know how his new choices would affect his future, but seeing that Keri had no recollection of the altered letter was proof that his new reality was definitely different. For her, his new reality was her *only* reality, and there was no *other* life. He wanted Keri to understand what was happening.

"Do you have *any* recollection, at all, of Rex changing the letter I sent you?"

"I'm not sure what you mean. You talked about Rex all the time, but the first time I met him was at our wedding, remember?"

That's right! She never married Rex. The first time she met him was at our wedding.

He examined the room more carefully. It was definitely not the same room in the Buckhead condo where he had fallen asleep. He played along, knowing she was not going to believe anything he told her about the *other* life—at least not now.

"That's right," he said, "I forgot. It wasn't until you moved to California that you had the pleasure of meeting the wonderful Rex Dean."

Like a fog burning off with the rising sun, the more distance he put between his dream and reality, the more aware he was of his life. He desperately wanted to see if she recalled anything from the *other* life, but he had to be careful how he worded his questions.

"Looking back, what would you say were some of the highlights that were special to you in the years that followed your move to California?" he said.

She squeezed his hand. "Being with you was all I cared about...and still do."

"Can you be more specific?"

"Isn't that enough?"

He put his arm around her and pulled her close, kissing her on the forehead. "You know it is. I feel the same way. But I was just wondering what special times or events stand out in your memory."

"Well...obviously our wedding at the Ritz-Carlton in Laguna Niguel was *the* highlight. It was any girl's dream wedding. I loved how you timed the ceremony perfectly with a beautiful sunset over Monarch Bay. High atop the bluff overlooking the Pacific Ocean, it was the perfect balance of elegance, serenity, and grace. And then there was the icing on the cake with a dream vacation to Hawaii."

He faked a puzzled look and said, "How long had you been in California before we were married...five months…six months?"

"Hmm…my transfer to L.A. was in July 1983, and we were married on Saturday, May 12, 1984, so that would make it nine months…no, ten months."

The fog in his mind had completely burned off. He was fully synced with the present. Even for him the details of their *other* life were slowly becoming a distant memory—a dream of what might have been.

In his current reality, he and Keri had been married for nineteen years, and he was an airline pilot living in California, not Georgia They had escaped the nightmare of the *other* life where he had once been married to the man-eater, Emily Anderson, and Keri to the womanizer, Rex Dean..

He said, "If you had to name one other event that stands out, what would it be?"

"That's easy, but it's actually not just *one* event, it's two." She smiled. "David and Martha, of course…the day they were born, August 31, 1988."

He laughed. "I guess you could call it two events. I agree, the greatest day in our life, other than our wedding day, was the birth of the twins."

When she mentioned the children, his mind ricocheted off his *other* life—a life replete with pain and struggle—where their deaf son, David, had been conceived in New York before they were married. But worse was the horrid night when Keri and the kids were held hostage, while the lunatic, Samael Janus, sent Ryan on a mission of death.

His body grew hot. Sweat beaded on his forehead. His heart began to race, pounding in his chest.

Oh no! If this is April 2003, then the night Keri and the children are taken hostage has not happened yet. That didn't happen until May 29th. That's next month!

"Honey, are you alright? Your face is beet red." Keri put her palm on his forehead. "You are sweating." She turned his wrist over and measured his pulse. "You'd better lie down."

As he put his head on the pillow he said, "I'm fine."

She got a damp bath cloth from the bathroom and placed it on his forehead. She took another pulse reading. "Almost normal now."

But wait! If this is April 2003, then the crash that occurred on July 11, 2002 should have already happened. If so, Rex Dean's wife, Emily, should be dead. Samael Janus murdered her that night.

In the *other* life, Rex Dean's jet was shot down on July 11, 2002. He knew for a fact it never happened. There had not been a major air disaster since 9/11. If that were the case, perhaps the horror of May 29, 2003 would never happen. But how could he be certain? He couldn't.

"Your color looks normal now and your pulse is fine. That must have been some dream."

"Yeah, trust me, it was a doozy." Ryan couldn't explain to Keri what really caused his sudden panic attack. To her, there was no *other* life. She knew nothing about a crazed lunatic threatening to murder her and the children.

The fragrance of the perfume had altered his future, not once, but twice. Interestingly, each dream regression into his past had taken him to an earlier time. First, there was his meeting with Keri in New York on April 1986—seventeen years ago. Choosing not to surrender to his lust in New York had spared him from the scars of sexual indiscretion and a son born out of wedlock.

Then there was his confrontation with Rex in May 1983—three years before his meeting with Keri in New York. Ryan had eluded being trapped by the self-indulgent woman, Emily Anderson, when he chose not to accompany Rex on one of his escapades to pick up women.

Those two moments had been critical junctions in his life where, in both instances, his original decisions had robbed him of many years of happiness. Because he had made different life-altering choices in both dreams, he woke to a new and much brighter reality.

If it were possible to experience one more dream regression to the time and place of his choosing, it would be in the circular drive in front of Keri's old home on June 23, 1974—the night she broke up with him before he left for the Naval Academy. If he could return to that night, he would be able to restore the hopes of all their dreams, but more importantly, he could ensure that the horrid events on the night of May 29, 2003, never had a chance of occurring.

Keri checked the time. "Oh, my! We need to get ready or we're going to be late for church. Do you feel like going?"

"I'm fine. I'll jump in the shower."

"I'll fix us something to eat."

While showering, he struggled to make sense of the two dreams that had literally changed his life.

Are the dreams connected?

Numbers whirled in his head; possible combinations that might lead him to a numerological association between the two dreams…anything.

Perhaps there is a relationship between the current year and the years in which the dreams occurred.

He subtracted the year of his first dream encounter with Keri in New York, 1986, from the current year, 2003:

$$\begin{array}{r} 2003 \\ -\ \underline{1986} \\ 17 \end{array}$$

Nothing special about the number seventeen.

Then he subtracted the year of his second dream regression to Rex's condo in Del Mar, California, 1983, from the current year:

$$2003$$
$$- \underline{1983}$$
$$20$$

Nothing special about the number twenty. What about the time between each dream.
He did the math:

$$1986$$
$$- \underline{1983}$$
$$3$$

The number three is a very significant number in the Bible.

The number three is often found to represent a period of separation, especially in the Bible: During the Creation, the earth was separated from the waters on the third day; the baby Moses was hidden in a basket for three days; Jonah spent three days in the stomach of a large fish; Jesus was missing from his mother for three days; Jesus was dead for three days before He arose on the third day.

If the year of the second dream was three years prior to the first dream, did that mean the time for all subsequent dreams would take place in three-year intervals? If so, the next dream should take him to some event in 1980; the next to 1977; and then, finally, to 1974.

Although the chance of another perfume-induced dream regression was beginning to sound a bit wacky, he dismissed the impossibility and continued searching for numerical associations.

He searched his memory for any decision he might have made during the years 1980, 1977, or 1974 that could have had a significant effect on his future life. Suddenly, like a treasure hunter stumbling upon the "mother-load"...

That's it! June 23, 1974...it was a Saturday night. It was the night Keri broke up with me. We were sitting in my '65 Impala in her driveway. I left for the Academy the next day.

Numbers spun in his mind like ping-pong balls in a lottery basket. He subtracted 1974 from the year of his first dream, 1986:

$$\begin{array}{r} 1986 \\ -\ 1974 \\ \hline 12 \end{array}$$

He could think of nothing special about the number twelve—alone, or when combined with the number three...except: $1 + 2 = 3$.

Although 1974 was twelve years earlier than his first dream, it also equaled three—the same as the number of years between the first and second dream. Then he subtracted 1974 from the date of his second dream, 1983:

$$\begin{array}{r} 1983 \\ -\ 1974 \\ \hline 9 \end{array}$$

The number nine is known to represent attainment or satisfaction. It is a number of finality or judgment...a number that represents the sum of all man's work.

The idea of a third dream being the final dream made the number nine even more perfect. Three multiplied by three equaled nine. His number theory would certainly appear ridiculous to most people, but to him it was clearly a sign, a code, a matrix—a confirmation—of what was to come.

He reviewed the numbers, so far. There had been three years between the two dreams. There were twelve years between the first dream in 1986 and 1974—the year Keri broke up with him in her driveway. Interestingly, the sum of the two digits, one and two, was also three. He played around with the numbers twelve and three. When he subtracted them: $12 - 3 = 9$.

Again, it was the number nine. He multiplied three and nine, thinking he would uncover a relationship between separation—three—and satisfaction—nine. The result was 27.

As he studied the relationship between three, nine, and twenty-seven, there it was again—the number nine: $2 + 7 = 9$.

Each time he spun the numbers, he saw new confirmations. Then something else popped out like a neon sign. Assuming the number two represented him and Keri, when it is joined with the number seven—the number representing spiritual perfection, fullness, or completion—the result is the number nine representing attainment, satisfaction, and finality.

He suddenly realized where he had heard the number 39; during a church service his pastor was teaching on the crucifixion of Jesus. According to the Old Testament, 40 lashes was determined enough to kill a man. Therefore, unless a man had been sentenced to death by flogging, the maximum number of lashes a flogger could administer was 39—the number of mercy according to Jewish law.

Mercy! A second chance! It's perfect!

Everything pointed him to the conclusion that an extremely high probability existed that his next dream regression, if it happened, would take him to the year 1974.

As his mind relentlessly continued to spin the numbers, searching for more possible confirmations, he made an unsettling connection with the number three.

The year of his second dream regression, the time when he was with Rex Dean in Del Mar was 1983. Not only did 1983 end with a three, when he added the numbers: $1 + 9 + 8 + 3$, the resulting number was 21. When he added the two numbers: $2 + 1$, it produced the number three. The number three represents separation. Rex had been the divider. Again, this made perfect sense.

He and Keri had always been meant for each other, but the divider—Rex Dean—had blindsided them with his deviously concocted plan and altered their destiny. Rex Dean had been the cause of his and Keri's separation. Everything associated with the events surrounding the second dream pointed to the number three—the divider.

Ryan and Keri—2—had always been destined to be together—7—and even though Rex Dean—3—came along and tried to separate them, in the end, attainment and satisfaction—9—was still realized: $27 \div 3 = 9$.

There was no doubt that he and Keri were destined to be together, but they would have been together much earlier if Rex had not concocted his devious plan.

By making a different choice in the second dream, I completely removed Rex Dean, the divider, from the equation leaving the simple equation: $2 + 7 = 9$. All of my lost years with Keri were restored.

If the numbers were pointing the way, his next dream regression would take him to the time and place of the last and most significant event in his life—Saturday, June 23, 1974—the date that matched the number nine; the number representing attainment, satisfaction, and finality.

I need to pick up a bottle of Angel perfume as soon as possible.

CHAPTER 10

Southern California
Sunday Morning—April 2003

*R*yan spent the entire week anticipating his trip to Nordstrom to purchase a bottle of *Angel* perfume.

On his way home from LAX on Friday afternoon, he stopped by South Coast Plaza. He had called and they had plenty in stock.

Three women were behind the counter in the cosmetic department. One was applying makeup to a customer seated on a stool, one was processing a purchase at the register, and the third woman, a tall red-head, had locked eyes with him long before he reached the counter, almost as though she was expecting him.

"How can I help you," she said. The woman's manikin-like face was pasty-white with rosy cheeks—skin easily mistaken for plastic or fiberglass. Her unnaturally-blue eyes must have been due to colored contacts.

"I called earlier and confirmed you had a perfume named *Angel*."

The mix of powders, perfumes, and lipsticks confused his sinuses. He prayed he would not burst into a full-blown allergic attack.

"The redhead pointed to a large display of assorted *Angel* perfumes at the end of the counter. "I'm not wearing it today, but *Angel* is a favorite of mine. It was the first perfume created by Thierry Mugler."

On the front of the box was the word ANGEL with Thierry Mugler's signature.

"Is this for your wife or someone special?"

"Ahhh…my wife."

"I'm confident she will love it. *Angel* is a very pleasant fragrance. It has a combination of praline and chocolate-derived sweetness mixed with a strong accent of patchouli."

"What is patchouli?"

"Patchouli is a musty, sweet, spicy, heavy scent. It is relaxing, uplifting, soothing and is believed to be an aphrodisiac. Patchouli oil has many beneficial effects, one of which is to relieve stress."

When he heard the word 'aphrodisiac', he instantly remembered the sensation of his first encounter with the fragrance when he passed the woman leaving Starbucks. Something drew him to her. "Sounds wonderful."

She continued with her pitch. "It evokes the emotion of tender childhood memories together with a sense of dreamlike infinity."

He looked at her. "Did you say 'dreamlike infinity'?

"I sure did. That's how the company describes the fragrance." She turned the box over so he could read the description on the back:

Dreams and fantasies come true with the celestial and delicious facets of ANGEL. The celestial facet is icy, like a draught of fresh air. Ethereal and transparent, it is a floating moment of pure softness. The delicious facet evokes childhood memories of sunshine and sweetness.

He laughed. "Wow, that is amazing! Absolutely amazing!"

I should have known.

She reached for a sample dispenser, but before she could press the plunger on the .08 ounce star-shaped bottle, he said, "Please! Don't do that."

"Wouldn't you like to sample it?"

"I'm allergic."

The redhead's painted-on eyebrows lifted, her porcelain-like brow furrowed.

"It's complicated," he said.

As she rang him up, she asked, "Would you like me to wrap it up?"

He glanced at her name tag. "Thank you, Grace, but this will be fine." He paid quickly, left the mall, and headed home with his *Angel*.

The description on the box said it all:

> *Dreams and fantasies come true... Ethereal and transparent, it is a floating moment...evokes childhood memories of sunshine and sweetness.*

His third dream regression into his past was certain to fix everything. The rest of their lives would be restored and their original purpose fulfilled. All of his failures resulting from poor judgment and the subsequent painful consequences would finally be purged. Any memories of the *other* life—if it existed—would be completely morphed into the unanswerable "what if", only to be remembered as a dream, including the horrid night of May 29, 2003, when Keri, David, and Martha almost died at the hands of an evil monster.

A satisfying calm relaxed him. He flipped on the radio. The announcer said, "Here is that 1997 hit by Sarah McLachlan, *Angel,* from her best-selling album, *Surfacing*."

"No way!" He turned up the volume.

A few soft piano chords introduced the ethereal ballad. McLachlan's smooth voice followed... "Spend all your time waiting for that second chance..."

As he listened, his thoughts drifted into his past as he followed the lyrics of the song. The powerful emotion found in the music transcended the songwriter's original theme, touching his life. He had always been a fan of McLachlan's music, finding it a soothing escape, but to hear this particular song at this time could only be the result of divine intervention.

Over the years, he had become more sensitive. The trials of life had softened his heart to the pains and joys of mankind. He even cried in movies when the hero overcame insurmountable obstacles to save the girl or the town.

By the time McLachlan had reached the last line in the first stanza his eyes were watery. Then she rolled into the chorus... "In the arms of the angel fly away from here..." His chest tightened. Tears spilled from his eyes. He could not contain himself. Almost every word she sang seemed directed to his situation.

When the song ended he turned off the radio, not wanting to spoil his blissful state; his heart full of joy and peace.

He pulled into the garage and tucked the *Angel* perfume into his flight bag. Keri greeted him at the door. "Did you have a good day?"

"I'm just glad we have a weekend for a little R&R."

And a bit of needed time travel.

"Me, too." She kissed him, pausing to look at his eyes. "Have you been crying?"

He rubbed his eyes, turning his head away. "No...I'm good."

"Supper will be ready in fifteen minutes."

"I'll be back in ten." He rushed upstairs to his bathroom

and hid the box of *Angel* in his medicine cabinet behind a can of shaving cream.

Tomorrow morning he would be at Starbucks by six o'clock, order a tall coffee, and ingest a healthy whiff of *Angel*. By this time tomorrow night everything would be perfect—finally free from all regrets and any chance of reliving the horrid events of May 29th.

Returning to the kitchen, he whistled the tune to Sara McLachlan's *Angel*.

CHAPTER 11

Southern California
Saturday morning—April 2003

*R*yan arrived at Starbucks at 5:30 a.m. in early-morning darkness. He stood by the entrance of the store as an employee fiddled with a handful of keys.

After unlocking the doors, the employee said, "Hi, Ryan."

"Good morning, Ashley." He moved to the counter. "Hi, John. I'll have a tall coffee, please."

He took his coffee to the condiment bar, added milk and sweetener, then found a seat near the window. He pulled the palm-size, star-shaped dispenser of *Angel* from his pocket. He patiently sipped his coffee observing customers.

When his cup was half empty, he sprayed *Angel* on the inside of his left forearm. He lifted his arm to his nose and inhaled. A slight burning sensation tingled the inside of his nostrils. The volatile top note, or first scent impression, was light and refreshing with a hint of sweetness. The middle note—the "heart note" as it is called—would follow in about ten minutes after the oils in the perfume fully developed on the skin and the top note had evaporated. He inhaled a second time.

Nothing yet.

It'll take a few minutes.

He took a sip of coffee waiting anxiously for a sneeze. Just to be sure, he pumped another squirt of *Angel* on his arm and drew in the fragrance. He waited approximately three minutes.

Nothing.

His heart raced.

I should be sneezing by now.

Concerned too much perfume would draw attention, he took his coffee and left the store. Sitting in his car he pumped the star-shaped dispenser a third time, sending a mist into the cabin of the car. He inhaled deeply and coughed. He waited a minute.

Still nothing.

I don't understand.

Frustrated, he tossed the bottle of *Angel* on the passenger's seat and started the car.

Grace must have sold me a dud.

He backed out of the parking spot and drove toward the exit.

I'd better get this stuff off or Keri will wonder why I smell like a woman.

He stopped the car and wiped his forearm with a Starbucks napkin. He sniffed his arm. The oils in the perfume were still emitting a strong scent of the fragrance. He took the napkin, spit on it, then rubbed his arm hard, until it was hot from friction and the napkin almost disintegrated. He sniffed his arm again. The scent of Angel was still strong.

I need something strong...some type of cleaning fluid.

He searched the car for anything he could use to rid him of the prissy-smelling fumes. Between the seats he found a small half-filled bottle of hand sanitizer. He squirted a liberal amount on his arm where he had previously applied the

Angel perfume and rubbed it back-and-forth with his hand. A strong scent of alcohol quickly replaced the sweet fragrance of the perfume. Once the sanitizer evaporated, he lifted his arm and sniffed his skin. It was clean and fresh—free from the fragrance of the perfume. He lowered the windows.

Turning onto the street, it hit him hard. "Ahhhhhh....chooooo!"

Now we're talking. Bring it on!

His eyes began to burn and itch, much worse than any of the other times.

Burn baby burn.

Tears flooded his vision making driving almost impossible. "Ahhh....chooo!"

Yeah...that's it. Sneeze your head off.

His nose dripped like a garden hose, but he managed to whistle the tune to *Angel* until he arrived back home. The house was dark and quiet. He headed straight to the bedroom where Keri was still in bed sound asleep and then into the bathroom. He washed his face and blew his nose. Thankfully, the sneezing had subsided. He was hopeful he could get back in bed without waking Keri.

"Is everything okay?" Keri said.

"Ahh...choo!"

"Are you getting sick?"

"No, I'm fine. I went down to Starbucks and I must've gotten a whiff of something I'm allergic to. I just need to lie here and sleep it off. I'll be fine in an hour or so."

She would not remember anything about his other allergic attacks leading to his previous two dream regressions, as they were not a part of her present—and only—reality.

"Okay, I think I'll go downstairs and let you sleep. Let me know if there's anything I can do for you." She closed the bedroom door as she left.

According to his numbers theory, he expected this dream

would take him to the year 1984—nine years earlier than his last dream. If so, it seemed only logical his dream maker would choose Saturday night June 23rd. That night had defined his future more than any other day in life.

As he relaxed, he imagined sitting in his 1964 Chevrolet Impala parked on the circular driveway in front of Keri's old home in Buckhead.

Sleep came quickly…

Where am I? This is not right. Where is Keri?

Ryan sat at the kitchen table drinking coffee. He was in the kitchen of a previous house where he once lived. It was early morning. The black of night was slowly yielding to twilight, releasing the once colorless world from its prison of darkness. He was in California. He was alone.

The TV was on, but muted. He picked up the remote and pressed the MUTE button and adjusted the volume to low. He took a sip of coffee.

A sense of gloom engulfed him before he could even process what he was seeing on the TV. The reporter was on location. A beautiful shot of the Pacific Ocean filled the background.

Ryan's heart thumped hard against the inside of his chest. More gloom accompanied by despair darkened his spirit.

I remember. It's the crash on July 11, 2002. Rex was the pilot.

The TV cameras zoomed in on the ocean. Rescue boats, rocked by ocean swells, searched through floating debris while helicopters circled above. The camera slowly panned the hopeless scene, occasionally zooming in on pieces of wreckage as the news reporter recapped:

"Late last night at approximately eleven-thirty, a commercial airliner departing Los Angeles International Airport bound for New York's JFK was shot down by U.S. fighter jets. We have been told that authorization to destroy the airliner was given after officials learned the plane was headed for a target in northern California. Numerous unsuccessful attempts to contact the pilots left officials with little doubt that the plane was under the control of terrorist hijackers."

He sipped his coffee, unshaken by the news, as though he expected it.

Keri rushed into the kitchen. "RYAN! DID YOU HEAR THE NEWS!?"

He calmly turned to her. "Yeah, one of our planes crashed last night." He took another sip of coffee.

"IT WAS SHOT DOWN! DID YOU HEAR ME? SHOT DOWN!"

I wish she would stop screaming. I can't enjoy my coffee.

He said without emotion, "I know...blew it out of the sky. Everyone died." He paused. "Listen, what did you have planned today? I thought we might drive out to the cemetery and put some fresh flowers on Rex and Emily's graves. How does that sound to you?"

Her tone had lowered just below a scream. "What! Are you crazy? What graves are you talking about?"

He pointed to the TV. "Theirs."

"Who?"

"Rex...and of course Emily...we can't forget Emily...after all, she was murdered last night. So, we should pick up enough flowers for both graves. I was thinking some carnations would be nice, or maybe some roses. We want to make it look nice."

"Ryan, you are freaking me out! What are you talking about?"

He pushed back from the table, moved to the coffee maker, and slowly poured a fresh cup of coffee. As he poured, he calmly said, "You'll see...just keep watching."

"Ryan...how do you feel?"

"Keri," he groaned, "I really need to sleep right now."

"Honey, you have been asleep for two hours. I just came to check on you."

He opened his eyes.

Where am I?

"Did you say two hours?"

"Actually it's been a little longer than that. I left the bedroom about six-fifteen and it's almost eight-thirty now."

I'm still in the same place and time.

"I don't understand."

"*What* don't you understand?"

He thought for a minute. "My dream."

Why was the dream in 2002 and not 1974?

"What was your dream about?" she said.

This is not good. The number theory didn't work.

"It was all wrong." He sat up. A part of him was still in Neverland. "I dreamed a plane crashed and somehow I knew Rex was the pilot of the plane. The same people responsible for the crash murdered Emily."

"Wow! That sounds like a night horror, not just a dream."

He looked her in the face. "It was *sooo* real, but it was all wrong."

"How can a dream be wrong?"

I can't explain it to her.

"*You* came screaming into the room...hysterical, while I sat calmly at the kitchen table drinking coffee. I didn't seem to be concerned about the crash at all. I don't understand."

She stroked his thick, brown hair. "I'm sorry you had a bad dream, but that's all it was…a bad dream."

"Are we still in California?" The moment he asked the question, he already knew.

"What do you mean 'are we still in California?'" Her voice sounded concerned. "Ryan, are you feeling alright?"

He forced a fake smile. "I'm fine."

"Well," Keri said, "you sound like you might still be half asleep. I suggest you stay in bed until you wake up." She stood. "Come join me when you wake up." As she left the room she said, "Don't forget, I'm cooking a big breakfast."

Unanswerable questions swirled in his head. He was still in the same reality as before he went to sleep? Why didn't he dream about 1974…and his last date with Keri? Why had he dreamed Rex died in the crash and Emily was murdered? He saw Rex at LAX last week and, unless something had changed, Rex was still married to Emily. Perhaps he had overdosed on the perfume?

Oh, no! What if the dream was not about what had already happened, but instead about what was about to happen? Instead of a corrective dream, the dark dream must be predicting the future.

His mind spun to the next logical point on the timeline of his future: the horrid night Keri and the children were held hostage by the white freak—May 29, 2003.

But it's all screwed up.

If Rex crashed a year ago in July 2002, he and Emily should be dead, but he knew for a fact they were very much alive.

Not only had his number theory failed, there was no logic to the new twist in the timeline.

The reason Rex had been flying that particular flight on July 11, 2002, was because he had traded trips with Rex. But the flight never happened. That is why Rex and Emily are still alive.

He was confused. Nobody had died. Or had they? Would they? When? Nothing made sense. He didn't know who, when, how, or where Evil would strike first, but something ominous darkened his spirit; something as real as real could be—a presence. A sense of death filled the room.

Please, God, don't let anything happen to my family.

CHAPTER 12

Southern California
Sunday morning—April 2003

*A*lthough Ryan wanted to believe the *Angel* perfume was somehow responsible for changing his past, his last nightmare had shed doubts on his theory.

Plus, the idea of time traveling in his dreams to a place in his past and making choices that would alter his future was *beyond* absurd. Any reasonable person would explain it as nothing more than double dreams or dreams within dreams. Nothing more than a subset of false awakenings in which he dreamed he had awoken from sleep while he continued to dream.

Regardless whether his experiences were real or imagined, he was not ready to simply blow them off as being false awakenings, double dreams, or dreams within dreams. The experiences were so strong and real he had to continue to experiment with the *Angel* perfume.

Perhaps the reason for his last dream being so different from the first two had something to do with the quantity of perfume he had ingested relative to the amount of caffeine he had consumed. During his years of fighting fatigue and insomnia, he had learned brain chemistry plays a major role in sleep performance. The proper mix of perfume and caffeine might be the solution.

After very little sleep, excited to continue his experiment, he returned to Starbucks with his *Angel* and a bottle of hand sanitizer.

Once he had his coffee, he returned to his car. When the cup was half empty, he sprayed the perfume on his forearm, and breathed deep, drawing the sweet fragrance into his lungs.

Within minutes, as he'd expected, he broke out in an allergic reaction—sneezing, red, itchy, watery eyes, and sinus drainage. On the way home his condition worsened, however this time, it was not as violent as the previous morning.

Entering the kitchen from the garage, he paused. Ahhh...chooo!"

Keri was at her usual place, drinking coffee and reading her Bible. "Another allergic reaction?"

"What can I say?"

"You might want to stay away from Starbucks for a while."

This time, in her *unaltered* reality, she had continuity between yesterday and today. The timeline of life had not been changed by his last dream; a sequence he hoped would be broken today.

"I know for certain it's not Starbucks that is making me sneeze."

"Since we have been in California, you have had zero problems with allergies. Maybe a little sniffle when the Santa Ana winds blow in from the desert, but never with the westerly flow from the Pacific."

"It's probably a perfume or something. Who knows? Ahh...choo!" He rubbed his itchy eyes. "I'll be in the bedroom sleeping it off. Wake me in time for church."

"Okay. Try keeping those dreams dialed down. Think of something fun and happy before you go to sleep. I've heard that our dreams originate from actual experiences in our past. So if you haven't been there, you can't dream it. That awful dream you had yesterday must have been an exception."

"I'll work on that. Choo!"

He completed the ritual in the bathroom and then headed for the bed.

'Dreams can only come from actual experiences in our past.' I hope that is not true.

Exhausted, his body started floating within minutes.

The background sounds of air blowing from cooling fans and hissing through vents in the cockpit engulfed him in a protective white noise.

I'm dreaming, but where am I? What is the date? Why is this happening?

He gazed out beyond the windscreen and into the still night. A wave of amnesia suddenly replaced his pre-takeoff anxiety. He had no memory of traveling to the airport. No memory of conducting the pre-flight planning. No memory of how he arrived at the end of the runway ready for takeoff. It was as if he'd been beamed from beneath the covers of his bed, transported to the Los Angeles International Airport, and dropped into the cockpit of a commercial jet waiting for takeoff.

OH NO! Keri! The children! They are being held hostage! The freak is going to kill them! It's May 29, 2003.

Before he had time to unravel his confused thoughts and any fascination he might have with mind paralysis or time travel, the voice of the tower controller crackled in his left ear. "Angel eleven heavy maintain three thousand, runway two five right, cleared for takeoff."

A sudden jolt of fresh adrenalin charged through his veins vaporizing his reflective state. His heart rate quickened. His muscles tensed. His pupils dilated for extra sight.

I need to get out! I need to go save them!

The jet rumbled and shook as the large turbofans underneath each wing whirled to life, sucking in air like two, giant vacuums. The monstrous machine rolled down the runway, slowly at first, then faster and faster until it broke free of Earth's hold and into the darkness.

His mind waffled back-and-forth between his pilot duties and his apparent lapse of memory. The dialogue between the air traffic controller and the copilot continued as the jet stair-stepped higher into the night.

"Angel eleven heavy turn left heading one eight zero."

"One eighty, Angel eleven heavy," the copilot replied.

Instinctively, his dream double reached up to the glareshield and dialed in one eight zero on the heading-selector knob, commanding the autopilot to bank the jet to the selected heading.

I'm shouldn't be here!

The silky-smooth air beneath the jet's wings masked the sensation of being hurled through the black of night at more than two hundred miles per hour.

Ryan's uneasiness morphed into fear. He tried to speak but couldn't find his voice. His mouth moved, but his words were muted. He was unable to engage the copilot in conversation, but he remembered his name, Chuck Smith.

Chuck! What's going on? Why am I here?

"What are you doing?" Chuck had one foot propped up and was reading a novel.

Chuck slammed the book closed after marking his place with a two-dollar bill. He admired the cover. "That was amazing! You will love the ending...caught me completely by surprise." He turned and looked at Ryan and said, "It all makes perfect sense, now." Ryan saw the title of the book:

Flight to Freedom.

BAM! BAM! BAM!

The cockpit door burst open and slammed against the wall. In a blur of bodies and flailing arms, two men charged through the opened door, screaming wildly, slashing the air with ceramic knives.

✈ ✈ ✈

"NO!!!!!" Ryan's body lurched. His eyes fluttered open in a frightened panic. Soaked in sweat, he jerked up on his elbow.

Keri rushed to the bed and held his hand. "Ryan, Ryan, its okay. You must have had a bad dream."

He sat motionless as his thoughts synchronized with reality. "That was weird," he said.

"Your shirt is damp." She pulled away from the wetness.

"I was flying and two attackers burst through the cockpit door. They were about to slice us with knives when I woke up."

"Strange."

"How long have I been asleep? It feels like only a few minutes." He glanced at the clock on the nightstand. "Impossible! I've been asleep for over an hour?"

"Yep, quiet as a baby until a few minutes ago. I was in the bathroom putting on my makeup when I heard you yell."

This is definitely not good. I don't understand why the perfume is not working.

The same eerie sensation of death—as the day before—filled the room. It lingered like a dark presence stalking a wounded animal.

"I need to get up," he said.

"Okay. We have about an hour before we need to leave for church." Keri returned to the bathroom.

The first two dream regressions had worked beautifully, yet the last two resulted in nightmares and no change in reality.

The one glaring difference was that the first two dreams had occurred after inhaling the perfume worn by the woman named Angel. The last two dreams were after he had applied the perfume on himself.

It must have something to do with who is wearing the perfume.

He went to his office and flipped on his computer. After a quick search on the Internet—*does perfume smell differently on different people*—his suspicions were confirmed. He located a paper written by a post-doctoral college student studying biology and ecological chemistry.

He learned that each of the components of a person's skin—fatty acids, fat, salts, sugars, proteins, fibers, and hair—binds the chemicals in perfume uniquely, releasing an individual scent.

It makes perfect sense that different smells could have a different effect on my brain, emotions, and possibly my dreams.

He Googled another phrase—*do smells influence dreams*. At an annual meeting of the American Academy of Otolaryngology, research was presented from a study—*The Impact of Olfactory Stimulation on Dreams*—conducted on fifteen healthy women in their twenties to measure the effects of odors while they slept.

Tubes were taped to the subjects' nostrils, linking them to olfactometers. The devices pumped constant streams of air into their noses while monitoring the subjects' brain activity. Once they reached the rapid-eye-movement (REM) stage of sleep when most dreams occur, a shot of scent was administered via the olfactometer for ten seconds: sulfuric scent of rotten eggs or the scent of roses.

The dreamers continued sleeping for another minute until the scientists woke them up and asked them to describe their dreams and rate the experience as emotionally negative or positive.

When using the unpleasant odorant, the emotional coloration of the dream was predominantly negative, while under stimulation with the pleasant stimulus, nearly all dreams had a positive coloration.

The study reinforced the known fact that the sense of smell is closely associated with the brain's limbic system which governs emotion and behavior.

An ear, nose, and throat surgeon attending the meeting stated: "We know there is a link between smell and memory, and now there seems to be a link between smell and the sleep centers of the brain."

Ryan stared out his office window surmising what he had learned.

I guess it's not really important that the perfume smells differently on me than it did on Angel...or anyone else. What is important is how the two different smells affected my brain's limbic system, emotions, and behavior while dreaming. One set of dreams was positive and the other negative—one offered me the opportunity for new life; the other warned me of impending death.

The research was interesting, but what he had experienced in his last dream was a long way from interesting—it was freaky.

He shut down his computer and sat thinking.

If I can find Angel, she can lead me into another positive dream experience. It worked twice before with her, and there is no reason to believe it wouldn't work again.

The problem would be finding her.

The changes that resulted from the choices I made in the dream regression with Rex in Del Mar put me in a different time and place. When I met Angel at the Starbucks in Buckhead, I was living in Georgia in 2004. I'm now living in California, and it is 2003.

Even if the woman was still living in Georgia, what were

the chances she frequented the same Starbucks?

She said she had been using the Angel perfume since it came out—almost ten years.

A bigger problem was convincing Keri he needed to go to Buckhead, Georgia, to find a woman he'd met one year in the future? If he didn't want to lie to her, his only option was to try one last time to make her believe the entire ordeal—everything: what the perfume did to him, the four dreams, and the woman named Angel.

If his last two dreams had been premonitions or warnings of what might happen in the future, then Keri needed to know how serious it was that he locates Angel. The crash had occurred in his *other* life on May 29, 2003. Time was running out.

CHAPTER 13

Southern California
Sunday afternoon—April 2003

*R*yan had three hours alone with Keri to untangle his conundrum while the twins were at the movie with friends.

Keri cleared the table, passing dishes and glasses to him at the sink. He rinsed, then stacked them in the dishwasher. The stream of warm water flowing over his hands helped relax his mind as he organized his thoughts.

Keri had no recollection of any *other* life. The only life she knew was the present. She had no knowledge of the mysterious powers found in the fragrance named *Angel*, and she knew nothing of the woman, Angel, from the Starbucks in Buckhead.

Although his last two dreams had not zapped him into another time and place, the events in those dreams appeared real and threatening. The report of the crash he saw on TV involving Rex Dean had occurred in 2002. But there had not been a crash in 2002. Rex and Emily were both still alive.

Why did I dream it if it did not happen?

The thought of the other dream made him nauseous.

Keri, David, and Martha were being held hostage by a deranged lunatic. The freak had threatened to kill them if Ryan didn't fly his jet into the Golden Gate Bridge in San Francisco at exactly midnight on May 29, 2003.

That's next month!

After clearing the final dishes from the table, Keri eased up behind him and slipped her hands around his waist. "Just me and you on a beautiful Sunday afternoon in Paradisea. We've got it all to ourselves. What would you like to do? You name it."

He closed the dishwasher door and turned to face her. He pulled her close, swirling his hands across her back. "Anything?"

"Anything," she said.

He kissed her on the neck. "Well... I can think of a thousand things we *could* do, but I really need to talk to you about something that's bothering me."

She stepped back, still holding his arms. "Okay. Where would you like to talk?"

"It's such a beautiful day, let's sit on the patio."

"Great idea." She took his hand and led him to the double glass doors and onto the patio. The air was fresh and clean with a hint of ocean. Purple bougainvillea, bird-of-paradise, and hibiscus bordered the manicured lawn.

He set the glider in motion with a rhythmic push from his foot.

Start with what she knows, and then tiptoe carefully across the minefield of the unknown.

"So what's troubling you?" she said.

"Do you remember when you said dreams can only originate from actual experiences in our past?"

"It's something I remembered from a psychology class in college. I believe it was a book written by Sigmund Freud...something like: *Dream Psychology for Beginners*."

"Sounds interesting."

"I hate to admit it, but of all the classes I took in college, I probably remember more from that class than I do any of the others."

"So...Freud didn't believe dreams could be about future events?"

"Well...he said there is always a connection between parts of every dream and some detail of the dreamer's life. It doesn't necessarily have to be an actual event. It might be something you thought about during the day."

He kept the glider in motion as he gazed out at the ocean in the distance. "Does that mean if I had watched a Rambo movie, I might be Rambo in my dream?"

"It includes whatever is in the dreamer's mind. My professor used the *Wizard of Oz* as a great visual example. The key characters in Dorothy's journey to Oz, which was actually a dream, were cast from people in her real life in Kansas."

He stopped the glider's motion and turned and looked at her. "That's right! The Wicked Witch was that mean 'ol lady on the bike who came and took Toto because he had bitten her."

"Her name was Miss Gulch. And the farm hands, Hickory, Zeke, and Hunk, played the Tin Man, the Scarecrow, and the Cowardly Lion."

"Wow! You must have taken notes when you were a kid."

"Not exactly. I studied the story and used it in a paper I had to write on Freud's book. The names just happened to stick in my head."

He put the glider back in motion with a slight push and focused on the ocean. "I remember when I was a little boy, back before VCRs, I would never miss *The Wizard of Oz*. It came on every year."

"I researched that, too. From 1959 to 1991, it was an annual tradition and was always presented as a special program."

"Those were some fun times." His mind drifted. His mom would call him in from playing to get his bath, eat supper, and put on his pajamas in time to watch the *Wizard of Oz*. The entire day was coordinated so he wouldn't miss a single minute.

"Anyway, that's why I encouraged you this morning to try and think of something fun and happy before you went to sleep. I didn't want you repeating the nightmare you had on Saturday morning. Obviously, based on this morning, you never found that happy place."

Releasing his thoughts of childhood memories, he snapped back into the present. "I was exhausted. My mind was unwilling to search for a happy place," he said.

"That brings up a question. Freud said that in every dream, the dreamer attempts to gratify a wish or desire. So what was it in those two nightmares that had anything to do with a wishful gratification?"

He contemplated her question.

No better time than now to launch into the unknown.

He turned toward Keri. His heart raced. "You're not going to understand what I'm about to say, but I really need you to believe me."

"What makes you think I won't believe you?"

Just tell her.

"We aren't supposed to be in California."

"What makes you say that? I mean…is there somewhere else we should be…are you thinking about moving?"

"This is going to sound weird, but I know what caused the allergic reactions. It was a perfume called *Angel*."

"Perfume? Even if it was a perfume, how did know the name of it?"

"I *bought* it."

"What! Why would you buy perfume unless it was for me?"

"This is really going to sound strange, so brace yourself."

"I'm ready." She held tight to the glider.

"Not only did the perfume cause me to have an allergic reaction, it also had a certain quality that affected my dreams."

"What kind of 'quality'?"

"I've had four very unusual dreams as a result of that perfume."

"Are you talking about those two nightmares you had yesterday and today?"

"Yes, but there were two more."

"I don't remember you saying anything about any other dreams."

"Well…I tried to tell you…that's what's bothering me."

"I'm not sure I understand."

He stopped the glider. "This is the part where you will think I'm going crazy. During the other two dreams, I was able to make decisions that have altered our present life…"

She turned sharply and stared, pausing briefly. She chuckled. "What exactly do you mean by 'altered our present life'?"

"Keri, I'm not kidding. The life we are living now has changed. I really need you to believe me."

Her face took on a worried look.

"Ryan, you are scaring me. Is this a joke?"

"You don't remember, but last weekend on Saturday *and* Sunday morning, I had two more dreams. I had just come back from Starbucks and I was having an allergic attack."

"Where was I?"

"You were there."

"If I was there, then why don't I remember?"

"Technically, 'there' is not here." He waved his hands around encompassing their current surroundings. "You…we…were actually in Georgia last weekend." He looked away, thinking. "Not literally last weekend, but a weekend very similar to it…one year in the future, in 2004."

She locked eyes with him in a deep stare, then broke into laughter. "Ryan Mitchell, you are too funny."

He remained serious. "I know it sounds crazy, but it's the truth. It's because of the perfume."

"Ryan, do you know how crazy you sound? Why are you acting so serious?"

"Keri, I know this all sounds ridiculous to you. It even sounds crazy listening to myself tell the story. But it really happened. The only reason we are still in California is because of the woman that started all this."

Keri's eyebrows lifted. "A woman?"

Ryan took her hand, "It's all about the perfume this woman was wearing. While we—you and me—were living in Georgia, I bumped into a woman in a Starbucks in Buckhead wearing *Angel* perfume. You don't remember it, but that was when I had my first allergic reaction. I went home that morning and slept…same as I've done the last…" He had to think. "…two mornings."

"I'm confused. Are you talking about what you did in your dream?"

"No! This actually happened!"

"Then why don't I remember it?"

"That's what I'm trying to explain!"

"Okay. Stay calm. I'm listening."

"In the first dream, I was in New York on a layover. You were there too. I was married to Emily…"

Keri interrupted. "Wait! Emily…as in Rex's wife, Emily? You were married to Emily Dean?"

"Yes, but stranger than that, you were engaged to marry Rex, the next week."

She laughed. "Wow! Ryan, you really should put this on paper. It would make great reading."

"I told you it would sound crazy."

"Ahhh…yeah…just a little."

"Hear me out."

She held a smile. "I'm sorry, please continue."

"Here comes the hard part."

She gripped the glider. "I'm ready."

Ignoring her playful disbelief, he continued. "During that dream, while I was in New York, I was presented with a choice. You asked me to go with you to your dad's Upper East Side condo. I knew that if I went, we would do things that we would regret for the rest of our lives. It was weird, but I *knew* what would happen in that condo."

"How did you know?"

"That's what's so freaky about the first two dreams."

"How could that even be possible?"

"All I know is when I woke up from that dream, our reality was different. We were living in a different world than the one before I went to sleep. And the weird thing is that after I woke up, I had knowledge of both lives and the differences between them. I knew that because of the decisions I had made in the dream, my real life had changed and the *other* life was only a dream."

She sighed. "There is a logical explanation. In my class, we had a section on double dreams, false awakenings, and dreams within dreams. What *you* are calling your *other* life, is actually only a dream within a dream. So when you woke up, all the things you think changed because of decisions you made during your dreams…were actually things that changed from one dream to the next—not in your real life."

"If so, how do you explain that you don't remember my first two allergic attacks, even though they occurred before I bought the perfume?"

"Simple. You dreamed it. I don't know what has been making you have these dreams or what they mean, but I can promise you—that's all they are…just dreams."

What Keri was saying made sense, but it all seemed too

real. He sat thinking.

Keri said, "So…I'm curious. What was our life like back in Buckhead? Were you still flying for the airline?"

"We left California after something horrible happened to us. Some crazy freak held you and the kids hostage and threatened to kill you if I didn't fly my jet into the Golden Gate Bridge. It all turned out okay, but after that, I quit flying and we moved back to Georgia. I got a job as a simulator instructor and we lived in a condo in Buckhead. I'm not really sure what happened next because when I woke up, we were back in California."

"You see! We never left. You just dreamed we did."

It's hopeless. She will never believe me.

In a monotone voice, he said, "I guess you're right."

"I love you," she said. She kissed him, then stood. "You make life so exciting. I'm going back inside and use this time to catch up on some reading while the children are gone. Is that all that was bothering you?"

"Yeah."

"You really should think about writing a story."

"Maybe so."

It was so much easier to simply believe it was all a dream than try and explain the weirdness. But something inside of his mind wouldn't let go. If he could find something in his present reality that should only exist in his dreams—an object or a person—he could prove that his *other* life was not merely a dream. Locating the woman named Angel would solve everything, but that would be nearly impossible.

I've got the answer!

Mercy Flight and Captain John Dross. The only place he had ever heard of that company or their chief pilot was while he was living in Georgia—in his *other* life. If he never lived in Georgia and it was only a dream, then Mercy Flight would not exist and there would be no chief pilot named John Dross.

He jumped up and hurried to his office. He pulled up Google. He typed: *Mercy Flight, Inc. Captain John Dross.*

I knew it!

The website of Mercy Flight, Inc. with a picture of a pilot, three men dressed in business suits, and a female flight attendant were standing beside a Gulfstream G650. In the caption under the picture he saw the name, Captain John Dross, Chief Pilot. It was the same man from his dream—or his *other* life.

He chuckled.

If Mercy Flight and John Dross are not merely figments from my dream, then there is the possibility the woman named Angel is also real. If his last two dreams— nightmares—had anything to do with his imminent future, he needed to find her fast.

I can't tell Keri...not now.

CHAPTER 14

Southern California
Sunday night—April 2003

*W*hile Ryan searched the Internet on his computer downstairs in his office, Keri shuffled through boxes in the upstairs, hallway closet. The closet had served as a tomb containing the few personal items they had kept belonging to Martha Mitchell after her death.

There it is.

She pulled a file box from the closet and removed the top. The box contained assorted file folders that were easier left buried in the dark closet: copies of her death certificate, a living will, a checklist for final arrangements, healthcare power of attorney, a receipt from the crematory, and a list of contacts.

She pulled the file from the box labeled CONTACTS. She opened the folder and scanned the single page inside, looking for the name of the assisted living facility in Laguna Beach where Martha had spent the last few years of her life battling Alzheimer's. When Keri found it, she jotted down the number on a separate pad.

She returned the box to the closet, closed the door, and

went to take a relaxing tub bath. While the tub filled, she adjusted the temperature of the running water, and lit a lavender candle. Steam engulfed the bathroom in a cloud of mist.

She pinned her hair up, undressed, turned off the water, and stepped into the tub. The warmth sent a soothing charge throughout her body, relaxing her down to her core. With only her head above water, she let her mind and body unwind with the soft stimulation of the pleasant fragrance.

Her conversation with Ryan earlier had troubled her. Something didn't seem just right. Even though he had agreed that his fantasy about living a double life was actually a dream, there were moments when his intensity during the conversation had frightened her. If something was wrong with him, he shouldn't be flying a jet all over the world.

She stepped out of the tub, toweled off, and applied a liberal amount of her favorite body moisturizing lotion over her smooth skin before slipping into her most comfortable pajamas. She brushed her teeth and headed to bed for a few minutes of reading.

"You know I've got a trip on Tuesday?" Ryan said, as he walked through the bedroom toward the bathroom.

"Where are you headed this time?"

He called out from the bathroom, "San Salvador. I'll be back on Thursday afternoon."

"Will you be off on the 20th for Easter?"

"Yeah, my next trip is not until Tuesday the 23rd."

The kids were too old for the Easter Bunny, but the family had always put a priority on being together for Easter.

She heard the spray of water from the shower and the shower door close. She adjusted her pillow and returned to her reading, but as her eyes passed over the words there was no comprehension. Her mind was on Ryan. He would be leaving on his trip Tuesday. In order to ease her mind about his condition, she needed to spend as much time with him as possible tomorrow.

Tonight she would ensure he was satisfied and without wanting, and if necessary, again tomorrow night. The world was full of temptations and regardless of his faithfulness to her, she wanted to make it easier on him.

Hearing the shower stop, she placed her book on the nightstand and switched off the lamp. She waited and listened, imagining him completing his nightly routine.

The bathroom went dark followed by the glow of a motion detector nightlight in the corner of the bedroom. She watched his silhouette cross the room. He was shirtless, wearing only his boxers. His dedication to a disciplined workout program and commitment to a healthy lifestyle had kept him from morphing into the typical aging profile of most sedentary men in their 50s.

As he slipped into bed, she rolled on her side to face him. She drew in the pleasant scent of soap, lotion, and toothpaste. The nightlight clicked off. She brushed her leg against his. His hand reached for her and touched her arm. Her stomach fluttered. He pulled her to him. She tugged on his boxers hinting for him to remove them. He did.

They kissed. His hands explored her back. Warmth filled her body. She was safe in his arms.

"Tonight I want to make certain you have pleasant thoughts before you enter that dream world of yours," she said. She kissed him with passion and then rolled on top of his hard body. With his help, she slipped off her top.

With his gentle touches, his hands continued to please her in all the right places.

"I wish I could take you with me on my trip tomorrow," he said.

"You can. Just wish it so and I'll be there with you in your dreams."

✈ ✈ ✈

After checking his flight schedule for the week, he was able to drop his next trip, giving him seven days off. He couldn't tell Keri about John Dross or about going to Atlanta. John was one of his links to prove that the *other* life was not just a dream.

He shut down his computer and headed for the bedroom. Keri was already in bed reading. "You know I've got a trip on Tuesday?" he said as he walked through the bedroom toward the bathroom.

"Where are you headed this time?"

"San Salvador. I'll be back on Thursday afternoon," he lied, followed by a nauseous feeling of betrayal.

"Will you be off on the 20th for Easter?"

"Yeah. My next trip is not until Tuesday the 23rd." He stepped into a hot shower. The warm water poured over his tight mind offering a few moments of relief. Hopefully, by the weekend he would know more. He planned to call John Dross in the morning to arrange a meeting.

He stepped out of the shower, toweled off, and slipped on a pair of boxers. He then flossed, brushed, and gargled, flipping the bathroom light off on the way to bed.

After easing into bed, Keri's foot rubbed up against his leg. He reached over and stroked her arm then pulled her close. The fragrance of her lotion was refreshingly intoxicating. She pulled at his boxers insisting he remove them. He did.

Electric currents surged through his body, arousing him. They kissed. He had never grown tired of her physically, finding complete satisfaction in her loving touch. She was always eager to satisfy his every need. Her soft hand held him and stroked him gently.

"Tonight I want to make certain you have pleasant thoughts before you enter that dream world of yours," she said.

She kissed him with passion and then rolled on top of him. He helped her pull off her top—her only piece of clothing. His hands explored the warm soft curves of her body. As he touched her, his body grew tight. His mind went numb as his craving for her grew. His heart raced anxiously. "I wish I could take you with me on my trip tomorrow," he said, thinking of his trip back to Georgia.

"You can. Just wish it so and I'll be there with you in your dreams."

CHAPTER 15

Southern California
Monday morning—April 2003

Ryan woke early and drove to Starbucks. It was six o'clock West Coast time, nine on the East Coast. He called Mercy Flight headquarters in Atlanta and asked to speak to Captain John Dross. They transferred him to the flight department.

"Hello, this is Captain Dross." His familiar voice was deep with a noticeable and distinct Southern accent. It was the same voice he remembered when Captain John Dross was his student in the simulator—one year in the future.

"Captain Dross, this is Captain Ryan Mitchell. I'm currently based in Los Angeles flying for Freedom International Airlines."

"What can I do for you, Captain Mitchell?"

"My hometown is in the Atlanta area and I'm planning to be back in town on some personal business this week. I wanted to see if there was a chance I might be able to buy you lunch one day."

"What did you say your name was?"

"Ryan Mitchell."

An uncomfortable silence from Captain Dross made Ryan question his last comment.

"I understand if you are too busy," Ryan said.

"You said you grew up in the Atlanta area, right?"

"Yes, sir. I'm originally from Buckhead." Ryan sensed Captain Dross was understandably a bit leery of some stranger wanting to meet with him, especially with the increased attention on security since 9/11. He tried coming from a different angle. "My wife is also from Buckhead. Her father hangared his company's Gulfstream IV out at Peachtree DeKalb Airport back in the late '80s."

"If you don't mind me asking, what was your father-in-law's name?"

"Hart...Ronald Hart. He passed away in 1987."

"Ryan, what day would be good for you?"

"Ahh...any day that works for you."

"You name it. I'm free all week."

"How about Wednesday?" Ryan said.

"Perfect. I'll look forward to it. If you need transportation or a place to stay while you are in town give my secretary a call and she'll take care of it."

"That's very generous but I've got it covered. Thank you for offering." He had to fight hard not to accept the offer for a free hotel and car.

"Ryan, I'll contact you Tuesday evening to coordinate the details. I have your cell number."

"Talk to you then."

They hung up. Ryan sat quietly processing what had just happened. The last few minutes of the conversation were unexplainable. After he mentioned Keri's dad, John Dross changed his tone. For some reason, Ryan's connection with Ronald Hart had not only opened the door for a meeting, but inspired Captain Dross to roll out the red carpet. Whatever the reason, the meeting was set.

Keri knew Ryan would be flying on Tuesday, but she

normally never asked where he was going or for how long he would be gone until the day of the trip. So instead of driving to LAX on Tuesday to fly to El Salvador, he would drive to John Wayne Airport and fly to Atlanta to meet with John Dross. Keri would never know the difference.

His three-day El Salvador trip was scheduled to return to LAX on Thursday afternoon. That would give him plenty of time in Atlanta.

In addition to meeting with John Dross, he wanted to visit the Starbucks in Buckhead where he had first met the woman named Angel. There was a good chance she would still be living in the area. Perhaps one of the Starbucks' employees might give him some information. Or better yet, if he showed up early on Wednesday morning, she might stop for a coffee on her way to work.

The hardest part would be lying to Keri. It hurt just thinking about it. The trust they shared was sacred. He continued to remind himself that he was lying because he loved her.

When he arrived back home, Keri was at the kitchen table drinking coffee and reading her Bible. "I should have brought you a coffee," he said.

"I actually prefer this," she said, pointing to her cup.

He raised his eyebrows.

"I see you are not sneezing," she said. "I guess you managed to avoid being attacked by the *Angel*?" She smiled.

"Yeah, I don't think I'll need *Angel* anymore."

At least not until I find the woman named Angel.

"Did you have any interesting dreams last night?"

He paused. "All my excitement was *before* I went to sleep."

She looked at him and smiled. "It's all about happy thoughts before you go to sleep. Works every time."

"I'm not gonna argue with that." He wanted to tell her about his meeting in Atlanta, but he couldn't. Knowing he was lying to her made him queasy.

After I meet with John Dross, I'll be able to explain everything to her...then she will believe me.

CHAPTER 16

Southern California
Tuesday morning—April 2003

*R*yan showered, dressed in his airline uniform, and departed for the airport at 7:00 a.m. But instead of driving to LAX, as he always did to start his trips, he detoured to John Wayne Airport. He had several choices of non-stop flights leaving out of Orange County to Atlanta, but he planned to take the first available flight with an open seat.

Regardless of which flight he took, the three-hour time change and the four-hour flight guaranteed he would arrive during the madness of Atlanta's rush traffic.

He touched down in Atlanta a little after 4:00 p.m. By the time he deplaned and picked up his rental car, it was almost five. With his airline employee discount, he was able to book a room at the DoubleTree Hotel for under $100. The hotel was only a few minutes from Buckhead Village.

After a grueling drive north through Atlanta, he exited the freeway. The area was comfortably familiar. His thoughts tangled between his growing up years and the more recent *other* life.

In his *other* life he had not lived in the ritzy and affluent Buckhead, but in a mid-rise condo complex on Pharr Road, just off Peachtree. The condo was only a few miles from the DoubleTree.

When he was young, he lived on one of Buckhead's nicest streets and attended Pace Academy. When his father died everything changed. Leaving his mother penniless, they were forced to leave Buckhead and move into a rental in one of Atlanta's less desirable neighborhoods. Regardless, he always considered Buckhead his home away from home; a place filled with memories of his growing up years—a time when he and Keri were first in love.

After checking into the DoubleTree, he took the elevator to the second floor. Just as he opened the door to his room, his cell phone rang. His heart raced. The number on the screen had an Atlanta area code. "Hello," he said.

"Ryan, this is John Dross. Have you made it to Atlanta yet?"

"Yes, sir. I'm looking forward to our meeting tomorrow."

"Ryan, I'll pick you up at eleven. That way we can avoid the lunchtime rush."

"Are you sure you don't want me to meet you somewhere?"

"Where are you staying?"

"I'm at the DoubleTree on Peachtree Road near Lenox Square Mall."

"I know exactly where you are. I think it would be easier if I pick you up. I'll be there at eleven sharp."

"I'll be waiting. See you tomorrow."

Ryan was amazed at John's continuous over-the-top hospitality: his call, his offer to pick him up for lunch, not to mention the offer yesterday to take care of his hotel and rental car. What's next? Offer to fly him back to California on the company's jet?

Tomorrow morning he planned to be at the Starbucks located next to Barnes and Noble on Peachtree Road when they opened at 5:30 a.m. That was where he first bumped into Angel—in his *other* life. It was a long shot that he would see her, but he had to try.

Thursday morning he would return to the airport and catch the first available flight back to Orange County. Hopefully, he would have enough facts to persuade Keri that the *other* world did exist—not only in his dreams.

CHAPTER 17

Buckhead, Georgia
Wednesday morning—April 2003

*R*yan waited in darkness at 5:30 a.m. in front of the Starbucks on Peachtree Road for the employees to unlock the door. The drive from the DoubleTree was only a few blocks, putting him in front of the store ten minutes before they opened. He didn't want Angel to sneak in and leave without him seeing her, so he made sure he was the first customer.

Finally.

"Good morning. What can I get you?"

"Tall coffee, please."

Customers trickled in slowly at first, but by 6:16 a.m. a line had formed. His instinctive memory should recognize the women named Angel, but he chose a seat close to the door to capture the smell of the distinctive fragrance as she walked by.

If she was for some reason not wearing the perfume, he had his bottle, just in case. He placed his hand on his right pocket for reassurance of the star-shaped bottle. However, squirting her with the fragrance might present a challenge.

He checked the time: 7:05 a.m.

Still no Angel.

He would stay until nine o'clock. If Angel had a job that started at nine, she would have made her Starbucks run by then.

At 8:15 a.m. the steady stream of customers had slowed. He approached the cashier with his empty cup. The employee said, "Would you like a refill?"

"Please." On the employee's green apron, Ryan noticed the embroidery: LEWIS—STORE MANAGER.

When Lewis placed the coffee on the counter, Ryan said, "How well do you know your customers?" He knew Starbucks took pride in building a sense of community in their coffee shops. Employees were encouraged to get to know the customers.

"I probably know most of the regulars."

"Would you happen to know a woman in her early-to-mid 40s by the name of Angel? She's an attractive brunette, pretty smile, average build. I'd say she's about five-six. Very friendly."

Lewis looked puzzled. "Well…I do know a woman named *Angela* that meets that description. She comes in practically every weekend…early."

"Have you ever heard anyone call her Angel?"

"Not that I can remember."

Ryan distinctly remembered the woman telling him that the perfume had her same name.

"Are you sure?" Ryan said.

"I'm fairly certain, but she does match that description."

"Do you know what kind of car she drives?"

"No. I've never really noticed."

A wave of dizziness filled his head. Perhaps it was the caffeine, but more likely because he wondered if the woman Lewis called Angela was his Angel. Maybe Lewis was confused. He sees so many people it would be understandable.

"I'm willing to take a chance it's the same woman," Ryan said. "If I leave a note, could you see that she gets it. I'm visiting in town and will be leaving tomorrow."

"Sure. She comes in almost every Saturday and Sunday morning." Lewis handed Ryan a piece of paper and a pen, and then turned to take a customer's order.

Ryan wrote:

Hi Angel,

> *You might not remember me, but we met on a couple of occasions here at this Starbucks. I was talking to Lewis and he said you still lived in the area. I grew up in Buckhead, but have since moved to California. I wanted to thank you for helping me with the perfume and hope one day to return the favor. Perhaps we will meet again soon.*

Ryan Mitchell

He folded the note and passed it to Lewis. Lewis put it in a Starbucks envelope and sealed it. He handed Ryan a business card. "My name is Lewis. Call me next week and I'll let you know if she got the note."

"Thanks, Lewis, I really appreciate it. My name is Ryan."

"Nice to meet you, Ryan. I'll be working this weekend, so I'll keep an eye out for her. I'll also mention it to the other employees."

This meant another trip to Georgia—another lie he must tell Keri.

This could go on forever. What happens if she is not here on the weekend he returns?

He checked the time: 8:50 a.m. He tossed his coffee cup in the trash and headed for his car. With plenty of time before John was due to pick him up, he decided to take a short drive around Buckhead before returning to the hotel.

CHAPTER 18

Southern California
Wednesday morning—April 2003

Keri had no legitimate reason to suspect Ryan was experiencing dementia or a mental problem, other than the one time on Sunday afternoon when he passionately insisted they had lived two separate lives—something he kept referring to as his *other* life. After she had suggested how it was easily explained as a dream, he appeared to agree. But knowing that the Alzheimer's disease has a strong genetic component, and Ryan's mother had suffered with Alzheimer's, Keri couldn't help but be cautiously observant of Ryan's behavior for early signs of the disease.

It was 9:30 a.m. The children were in school and Ryan was in Central America. If she talked with someone at Ocean View in Laguna, maybe it would ease her mind about Ryan. Instead of calling, she decided to drive to the facility and speak with someone in person.

✦ ✦ ✦

Ocean View was where Ryan's mom had spent her last few years. Keri was familiar with the place, as either she or Ryan had visited Martha every day.

"Hello, Keri," said a familiar voice.

Keri turned to see a short, heavy-set, Hispanic woman in her 60s. She was the nursing assistant that had been so special to Martha.

"Ana-Maria! How have you been?"

"I've been fine…right here where you last saw me. How is Ryan?"

"He's doing good…" She paused.

Ana-Maria was the perfect person to talk to. She had been working in the Alzheimer's wing at Ocean View for over twenty years. If anybody understood dementia and Alzheimer's, she did. In addition to her many years of experience, Ana-Maria had also received her Certified Dementia Practitioner (CDP) certification.

"Actually, that's what I wanted to talk with someone about, and you are the perfect person," Keri said.

"Is something wrong?"

"I'm not sure." Keri's eyes filled with tears.

Ana-Maria took Keri's hand and led her into a nearby vacant room and closed the door. Her face showed a caring concern. "What is it?"

"Is it possible for someone with early stages of dementia or Alzheimer's to have confusing dreams?"

"Since dreams are stored in our long-term memory, if a person with dementia and short-term memory loss is reminded of something from a dream, they can think they have experienced it in real life, giving them an eerie feeling of déjà vu."

Shivers crawled up Keri's back like a spider. Her heart raced. She remembered how serious Ryan was about his idea of his *other* life. Water filled Keri's eyes.

Ana-Maria put her arm around Keri. "Honey, what's

wrong?"

"It's Ryan." She sniffled and wiped her cheeks. "I'm worried. I know it's probably nothing, but I just don't know."

"Is he acting strange?"

"It was just one time. He told me about a dream he had...well, it was actually more like another life he had lived. It sounded like he was confused, but he really believed it. After we talked for a while, he seemed to accept that it was only a dream. That was Sunday afternoon. Everything has been normal since then. He's on a trip now."

"I don't think I would get too worried about it right now."

Ana-Maria's words sounded hopeful.

"You think he's okay?"

"We have all been somewhere and had a moment of déjà vu. At least I know I have."

"Now that you mention it, so have I."

Ana-Maria said, "Our long-term memory is relatively permanent, able to store events as far back as when we were five or six. For Alzheimer's patients, short-term memory usually goes first and is followed by their long-term as the disease progresses."

"But what about the déjà vu? Ryan was persistent about trying to connect our present life with the events in his dream. He believes things happened that didn't."

"As the short-term memory starts to disappear, the long-term memory is often perceived as the patient's current reality. But this is after the disease is fairly developed. I really don't think this relates to what Ryan is experiencing."

"Ana-Maria, do you think I should be worried? Be honest."

"No. Not simply because he had a déjà vu experience. Like I said, that is perfectly normal."

Keri hugged her. "Thank you. You have made me feel so much better."

"If you have any other concerns, please call me...or better yet, come visit. I love seeing you. I forgot to ask, how are the twins?"

"They are almost grown...or at least *they* think so." Keri turned to leave. "I know you are busy, but thank you for your time."

"Tell Ryan and the children I said hello."

"I will."

During her drive home, the peace that had left her on Sunday afternoon returned. Everything was normal. She was not losing Ryan to the dark world that imprisons the mind. She was anxious for him to return from El Salvador. She wanted to hold him in her arms and hear his voice. The thought of him trapped in some boring hotel in a foreign country made her sad.

Ryan, wherever you are, I love you.

CHAPTER 19

Buckhead, Georgia
Wednesday noon—April 2003

*R*yan paced in the lobby of the DoubleTree Hotel waiting for John Dross to arrive. So far, the trip to Atlanta had been a big success. He was minutes away from meeting with John Dross, and it looked highly probable he had located Angel. His thoughts ricocheted between questions he wanted to ask John, and plans to come back to Buckhead to see if Lewis's Angela was the same woman named, Angel, he had met one year in the future in his *other* life.

Ryan stood by the door to the lobby. John was in his late fifties, about six foot two, lean build, mostly grey hair, and a strong jaw. He should be easy to recognize.

He looked down at his watch to check the time: 11:00 a.m. When he lifted his head, a black Lexus RX 300 was parked under the glass-covered canopy drop off. The man driving matched the description of John Dross. He made eye contact with Ryan and smiled.

Ryan hurried to the car and opened the passenger door. "Captain Dross?"

John reached and shook Ryan's hand. "Hop in Ryan."

"Thank you for picking me up."

"My pleasure. Do you have any druthers for lunch?"

"Anything is fine with me."

"You like fish?"

"Sounds great."

"Are you familiar with Atlanta Fish Market?"

"Is that the one with the giant fish out front?"

"That's the one. How can you forget a three-story sculpture of a copper fish?"

"I've never eaten there, but it sounds fantastic."

John turned with a puzzled look on his face. "How long ago did you say you lived in Buckhead?"

"I left for the Naval Academy back in 1974, and have been gone since then."

"They relocated to Pharr Road in 1993—long after you left. It's a popular place. Great food and excellent service."

"Sounds perfect."

John took Peachtree to Pharr Road and was in front of AFM in less than ten minutes. Ryan stared up at the copper fish. The only way he could have possibly known about AFM was when he and Keri lived in the condo on Pharr Circle after they moved to Georgia from California in 2004—in his *other* life. How else could he explain remembering a giant, copper fish? He would have had to drive by the big fish on many occasions.

They entered the restaurant through an antique wooden revolving door and were greeted by a hand-cut and laid mosaic in a fish scale pattern at their feet. Interior art deco lighting fixtures, wide plank hardwood floors, and high ceilings with open space enhanced the feel of warmth, relaxation, and nostalgia. Unique 1950's lighting fixtures, "funky wallpaper" with mermaids and tropical fish, sheet rubber floors, huge wall face clock, and a traditional porch with rocking chairs created a distinct New England mid-century charm.

"Two for lunch?" The hostess said.

"Yes," John said.

The hostess seated them in a booth and handed them menus. "Your server will be with you shortly."

Ryan flipped open the menu, skipped the teasers, and headed straight for the ENTREE SPECIALTIES. His eyes locked on the *Baked Atlantic Salmon Parmesan Crusted*. It came with grilled asparagus, and a crispy basil potato cake. He closed the menu.

"That was fast," John said.

"If I keep looking I'll want it all."

He was eager to pull back the curtain on John's over-the-top hospitality which began when Ryan mentioned that Ronald Hart was his father-in-law.

John closed his menu. "I'm ready."

A server stepped up and took Ryan's order first then turned to John. "I'll have the *'Favorite' Georgia Mountain Rainbow Trout with the Whipped Sweet Potatoes, Spinach, Macadamia Honey Butter.*"

"Excellent selections, gentlemen." She took the menus.

As Ryan considered how to begin the conversation, John said, "Ryan, I don't believe you are aware of the relationship between Mercy Flight and your father-in-law."

"Funny you should bring that up, I was about to ask."

"Mr. Hart was an amazing man, as I'm sure you know."

"Yes he was, and I loved him like a father. I could never repay him for all he did for Keri and me." Ryan reflected back on the miracle that brought Keri back to him. Ronald Hart had beautifully choreographed their reunion.

"Neither can I," John said.

"You?"

"When you called on Monday, it was as if I had been given the opportunity to travel back in time and relive my memories of him. Plus, I wanted to be sure you knew what he did."

"I can't wait to hear."

"Most men in Mr. Hart's position are poisoned by power, pleasure, and money. They have no concept of anything outside of their worlds; their worlds consisting only of one thing—themselves. The Proverbs even tell us that when fools grow rich, the Earth groans under them as they are a burden it cannot bear."

John must be a man of faith to reference the Bible.

John continued, "Most good men who seek power and fortune say they would think of others if blessed with such, but I dare say few would. Ronald Hart understood what was important and stayed focused. He recognized and accepted the great responsibility that comes with great blessing."

"He definitely lived with a passion for the purpose for which He was created."

John said, "Do you remember in our phone conversation when you mentioned Mr. Hart hangared his Gulfstream at Peachtree DeKalb Airport?"

"Keri and I actually flew to Hawaii for our honeymoon in that jet."

"I know."

Ryan threw back his head. "How would you know?" He smiled and chuckled.

"Because I was the pilot who flew you and Keri to Hawaii."

"No way!"

"After the limo dropped you guys in front of the jet, my copilot stood at the bottom of the stairs to greet you and see that your bags were loaded. I watched from the captain's seat. If you'll remember, as you were boarding, you stuck your head in the cockpit and said hello. You probably didn't get a good look at me, but even if you had, you would never remember me. Your mind was on other things."

Ryan tried to remember the details, but John was right, Keri was the only thing on his mind at that time. John could have been wearing a gorilla suit and Ryan would have never blinked. "So…how did you end up flying Mr. Hart's jet?"

"I was working for Gulfstream as a pilot in the sales department when he bought his first jet. He liked me from the start and offered me a deal I couldn't refuse. He was very picky about who he trusted. I'm sure you remember his lawyer…"

"Mr. Darby?"

"Phil and I were pals. Another great man. Your father-in-law had a knack for discerning character and used that gift to surround himself with great people. To be honest, that's why he was so fond of you. After Mrs. Hart busted you and Keri up, he was determined to get you two back together."

"This is starting to sound like you might know more about me than I thought."

"When you called me on Monday, I couldn't believe I was talking to 'the' Ryan Mitchell…Mr. Hart's son-in-law. Finally, when you said Ronald Hart was your father-in-law, I knew it was you." John laughed. "You'll have to admit that Mr. Hart's plan to take care of Emily and Rex was genius."

"You knew about that, too?"

"Who do you think was flying Emily all over the place: back and forth between Dallas and Atlanta, to New York, to California, or wherever Mr. Hart wanted her next. I also had to run a few trips taking little Miss Candi from place to place, making sure she was in the right place at the right time to meet up with Rex."

"This is mind blowing."

"I could talk for hours about everything Mr. Hart did for other people. He used his power and money mostly for the good of others. That is what made him such an amazing individual. God really found a true servant with that man— always putting together a plan to help others." John turned and looked Ryan in the eyes. "He loved you like his very own son. I wish you could have known him better."

"I do, too."

"There's one more thing you should know," John said. "Mercy Flight, Incorporated was Mr. Hart's baby."

"Really?"

"He dreamed it up, funded it, and made sure we would never need to beg for money. He wanted Mercy to be his legacy."

"He must have done that before Gold Street Capital cleaned him out."

"Mercy Flight was a completely separate entity. Mr. Hart wanted to make sure that regardless of what happened to his fortune, Mercy Flight would continue to 'fly', as we like to say."

"Well, as I'm sure you know, Keri and I lost everything Mr. Hart had intended to leave us, but this is the best news I could ever hear. It makes me feel good knowing a piece of him lives on, continuing to do the work that defined him—helping others."

"Ryan, the one hundred million you and Keri were meant to have was only a drop in the bucket. Mr. Hart was smarter and wiser than you think. He left most of his fortune to his charity."

"You mean the same charity that funds Mercy Flight?"

"That's right."

"I should have known he would do something like that."

Why didn't John contact Keri and me and tell us about all this? It's been over fifteen years.

The server arrived with their meals and placed them on the table. "I'll be back to check on you in a minute. Enjoy," she said.

"This looks great," Ryan said.

"There's nothing like fresh fish."

After his first bite, Ryan said, "I've got a technical question for you."

"Shoot."

"Didn't you fly us to Hawaii in a Gulfstream IV?"

John paused. "You and Keri were married in May of 1984, so Mr. Hart would have been flying the G-III. That was the best they had back then. We didn't pick up a G-IV until 1987. We have always been one of the first customers in line to upgrade to the new models. Mr. Hart only wanted the best.

May of 1984? That's right!

In his *other* life, before the second dream regression to Rex's condo, he and Keri were married in July 1987. So in that case John would have flown them to Hawaii in a G-IV. After he changed things in the second dream, he never met Emily Anderson on the beach at the Hotel Del Coronado and his letter to Keri was mailed before Rex messed with it. Keri moved to Laguna Beach in July 1983 and they were married ten months later on May 12, 1984. So instead of a G-IV in 1987, John had flown them to Hawaii in a G-III in 1984.

His thoughts ricocheted from one wedding to the next...1987...1984...1987...1984...both fresh in his mind, while details from his *other* life attempted to blur reality.

Ronald heart died in April 1987, three months before he and Keri were married in their *other* life, but he was alive on May 12, 1984.

Of course he was! He was at the wedding...with Barbara Ann.

The thought of Barbara Ann flipped his stomach like a pancake on a hot griddle. The woman was a witch. In his *other* life, Barbara Ann Hart had died in a car crash on West Paces Ferry Road in April 1986. On the day she died, she was returning a purse to one of her gossipy lady friends who had attended Keri and Rex's wedding. It must have been payback when the drunken redneck in the pickup truck crossed into her lane. She always did have it in for those "rednecks" in their pickup trucks. Ryan had a hunch that Barbara Ann might have been a little tipsy herself—as she often was—when the redneck took one for the team.

In reality, Keri never married Rex. Barbara Ann died a year after Ronald in February 1988 when she slipped on the icy steps leading up to her Buckhead mansion and hit her head on the corner of a brick—killing her instantly. Ryan called the one year Barbara Ann lived—after Ronald had died—his dark year. Up until the brick cracked her skull like a watermelon falling off a truck onto a hot asphalt road, Ryan was the brunt of her constant emotional abuse.

Ryan saw how every choice he'd made resulted in a domino effect of changes—not only in his personal life, but in the lives of everyone around him. The end result of his decisions had far-reaching effects on the people he loved and even people he didn't know.

John's enthusiasm grew as he kept talking. "We operate G550s now and as soon as the new model is announced in a couple of years, we will put our name on the list."

"That is awesome."

"You will love the G550. I can't wait for you to take a ride."

"Take a ride?"

"How does tomorrow sound?"

"What do you mean?"

"Didn't I tell you? I'm flying you home tomorrow."

"Are you kidding? How can you do that?"

"Before Mr. Hart died, he made sure I understood that if our paths ever crossed, that I should do anything possible to help you. Like I said, he was all about helping others—especially his family."

What did he mean… "if our paths ever crossed"?

"That sure is an expensive gesture to fly me all the way to California and then return empty."

"I'll never forget that conversation Mr. Hart had with me. It was after he knew he didn't have much longer to live. He said, 'John, I founded Mercy to help others, but if the circumstances ever arise that you get the opportunity to help

Ryan, Keri, or any of their children, I want you to do so. I mean anything, including the use of the flight department. Family always comes first. It almost makes you think that he knew you and I would meet one day.'" John laughed out loud and looked up at the ceiling. "Or maybe he is continuing to do his good deeds from Heaven."

I wish someone had told us. We could have used some help.

They finished their meal and John graciously picked up the check.

Back at the hotel, as Ryan exited the Lexus, John said, "What time do you want to blast off tomorrow? You name it."

"You tell me what works best for you. I'm still in a daze that you are doing this."

"How about I pick you up at ten o'clock so we don't have to hassle with rush traffic. We should be wheels up by noon and touch down at John Wayne by one o'clock, West Coast time."

"That sounds unbelievable. I'll be standing on the curb at ten sharp."

"See you then."

Ryan said, "Wait! I forgot. I've got a rental car. I'll need to drop it off at Hartsfield."

"That's ridiculous. I'll take care of it. Just leave me the keys."

"I can't ask you to do that."

"Ryan. Do I have to remind you? When Mr. Hart said *anything*, he meant it."

"Okay, whatever he says."

"Have a great afternoon and evening. I'll see you tomorrow." He drove off.

Ryan reflected back to his *other* life within his dreams when he first met Captain John Dross. It all made sense now. John had offered him a job because of Mr. Hart's request to 'do anything possible' to help him.

But that day was in his *other* life in 2004—one year in the future.

This is going to take some time to unravel. How can I ever explain this to Keri? Or should I even try?

He could hardly get his own mind around it. His heart grew heavy at the thought of her. He missed her desperately and hated thinking about having to lie to her.

He remembered Lewis at Starbucks and the woman named Angela. After his lunch meeting with John, the idea of being hurled into another allergy-induced dream regression— resetting his present reality—didn't sound so wonderful anymore. What happens if things don't turn out so pretty? Like a stone skipping across the surface of a pond, or a spacecraft attempting reentry too fast or too steep and finding a fiery end, he might wake up and find that everything good in his life has vaporized into his *other* life, trapped within his dreams?

Am I dreaming now?

CHAPTER 20

Buckhead, Georgia
Thursday morning—April 2003

Ryan woke as excited as a four-year-old on Christmas morning. His trip to Atlanta had paid off big. He had confirmed that John Dross, and possibly the woman named Angel, were living in his present reality, not merely illusions trapped within his dreams. He now had proof his *other* life did exist.

In addition, the news about Ronald Hart's connection with Mercy Flight and the provision he had made for Ryan's family was life-changing. As soon as he cleared his schedule, he and Keri would definitely return to Atlanta on a weekend to see if Lewis's Angela was his Angel.

He showered, dressed, and packed. There was no need to wear his airline uniform, as he planned to tell Keri everything once he arrived back home.

"Was everything satisfactory, Mr. Mitchell?" The desk clerk asked as Ryan slid his room key across the counter.

"Could not have been better."

After keying in a few computer entries, the desk clerk said, "It looks like everything's been taken care of."

Ryan said, "I assume you'll be leaving that on my credit card?"

"Ahh...no, Mr. Mitchell, someone from your company called this morning and paid your entire bill. We won't need to charge your credit card."

"Would you confirm for me the name of the company?"

"Mercy Flight, Incorporated."

Ryan smiled. "Thank you."

How could life get any better? Everything he and Keri had lost was being returned to them tenfold—possibly twenty, or even fifty, who knows. He checked the time: 9:15 a.m.

He used the forty-five minutes to grab a light breakfast and coffee in the hotel's restaurant, and then returned to the lobby to watch for John.

John drove up at exactly ten o'clock sharp, as though he'd been in a holding pattern carefully timing his arrival. He met Ryan at the rear of the car, shook hands, and lifted the tailgate. "John, thank you for covering the room charges."

He shot Ryan a quizzical look. "I can see this is going to take you some time to get used to." He tossed Ryan's roller bag into the back and closed the tailgate.

"I'm sorry, I guess I'm still in shock."

John put his hand on Ryan's left shoulder. "If you're in shock now, we might better call ahead and have the ambulance meet us in Orange County." They both laughed.

They arrived at Peachtree DeKalb Airport in less than thirty minutes. After keying a series of numbers into a keypad, the security gate rolled back. John wheeled up next to a large hangar and into a private parking space marked: CHIEF PILOT. He retrieved Ryan's bag, and entered the hangar through a nearby door covered by a maroon-colored canopy.

"There she is. Isn't she beautiful?" John said.

The Gulfstream 550 was in the hangar connected to a

tug. The hangar doors were open. "Very nice."

Ryan had a hard time processing what he was seeing. He ranked it somewhere between a dream and an out-of-body experience. Being flown from Atlanta to California in a fifty million dollar private jet, alone, was ridiculous.

John said, "My son, Michael, will be flying copilot for me today. He's been with us for about five years; one of our best. Obviously I'm proud of him…and a bit prejudice."

"That's fantastic! You should be."

Michael was John's copilot in the simulator.

"Michael should have the jet preflighted and ready to go. I'll just take a quick look at the weather and we'll be on our way."

While John checked the weather, Ryan stopped by the men's room.

Unbelievable!

Designed with an aviation theme, everything was first-class and immaculate. Marble floor, a wall-mounted flat screen TV showing the national weather, artwork, hand towels, and even mouthwash and lotion.

After leaving the bathroom, he followed John into the hangar and to the jet. Michael was waiting at the bottom of the stairs. "Michael, I'd like you to meet Captain Ryan Mitchell."

Ryan shook hands with Michael. "The pleasures all mine," Ryan said.

"Ryan is Mr. Hart's son-in-law," John said. Michael appeared to be impressed, as though he was shaking the hand of royalty.

They boarded the jet while it was still in the hangar. After the stairs were retracted and the door closed, the tug operator slowly pulled the jet from the hangar.

"Make yourself at home," John said as he and Michael entered the cockpit. "You're welcome to sit up here on the jumpseat or in the back for takeoff…your choice."

"There will be plenty of time later for a tour of the cockpit, I believe I'll find a seat in the back and act like I'm somebody important."

The interior was luxuriously appointed: fourteen soft, tan-hued leather executive seats; hand-rubbed wood inlays with Brazilian mahogany maple surfaces polished to a mirror-like sheen. Panoramic oval windows showered the cabin with plenty of light. At the rear of the cabin, a shiny mahogany door opened into a private sleeping quarter complete with lavatory and shower.

Ryan took a seat, buckled up, and enjoyed his new world. The engines spun up, they taxied to the runway, and within ten minutes were airborne.

The jet had been catered for lunch with an amazing spread of meats, fresh breads, veggies, and an assortment of fruits. After lunch, he spent an hour or so with John getting a tour of the Gulfstream's high-tech cockpit. He had time before they began their descent for reading and a short nap. The level of comfort and luxury he experienced was on the opposite end of the scale of what one experiences on a typical commercial flight.

The trip back to California went quickly—almost too quickly. John made a smooth touchdown at John Wayne Airport and taxied to Signature Flight Support. After they deplaned, Ryan said, "That was amazing. I'm still having a hard time processing what has happened since I met you."

"If there is anything you need, let me know. We are zipping back and forth all the time. Be glad to give you a lift…or for you…I'll even make a special trip."

"John…" Ryan paused.

"Don't say it," John said. "Remember—anything."

"Okay. I understand, *finally*. Are you headed back to Atlanta tonight?"

"We'll take a short break and then be on our way. Should be back by 8:00 p.m. local—5:00 p.m. your time."

Ryan reached to shake John's hand, but John opted for a man-hug and a pat on the back instead. "We're family now," John said. "I hope you will give me a call when you plan to come back and visit...or when you need to go anywhere else."

"I was hoping to get back over to Atlanta and visit my mom's old place on the first weekend I can get off. I thought Keri would enjoy seeing Buckhead. She hasn't been back in years—at least since she moved to California."

John handed Ryan a business card. "Call me. All I need is a day's notice. Unless I already have a trip booked for Mercy, I'll be more than happy to give you and that sweet wife of yours a lift."

Ryan looked at the business card and had a déjà vu moment. It was the same simple card he remembered from his *other* life—when John was his student in the simulator.

MERCY FLIGHT, INC.
CAPTAIN JOHN DROSS
CHIEF PILOT
770-552-1015

"I'll talk to Keri and then give you a call."

"Fantastic! It will be great to see Keri again. I haven't seen her since the flight to Hawaii for your honeymoon."

"Do you think she will remember you?"

"She should. When she was young, I hauled her and Mrs. Hart all over the world shopping. I flew them to New York practically every month."

"I'll give her your regards and talk with you soon."

Ryan headed for the parking garage.

Keri knows John Dross.

He'd never had a reason to connect these new dots. On the night of their honeymoon, Keri would have known that John Dross was the pilot of the plane flying them to Hawaii.

It was Ronald Hart's plane, and John Dross had always been Hart's personal pilot—the same pilot that had flown Keri and Barbara Ann on numerous shopping trips all over the globe when Keri was growing up.

Oh no! If Keri knows John, that means I can't use him to prove that the other life is real. As far as Keri is concerned, John has always been around, regardless if I only knew him in my other life.

This put a big kink in his plans. Telling Keri about his trip to Atlanta—or anything else—was now out of the question.

When he arrived at his car, he dug into his suitcase and pulled out his airline uniform. He would have to make it look like he was returning from his trip. He opened his car door and used it as a curtain, changed pants, and then put on his uniform shirt and tie.

Until I find Angel, I can't tell Keri anything. My next trip back to Georgia will be alone...which means I'll have to continue living this lie.

CHAPTER 21

Southern California
Thursday afternoon—April 17, 2003

Keri relished every day she had with Ryan as a gift not to be taken for granted. As an airline pilot, he spent half of his life away from home. They compensated for his fragmented schedule by spending as much time as possible together when he wasn't flying. It might be at a school event supporting one of the twins, or a simple walk on the beach. Regardless of the activity, it was all about multiplying the time they had together.

Tonight, she wanted to make everything perfect for his arrival. Even though he traveled weekly, anticipating his return always gave her a fresh excitement. She expected him home at about three o'clock, depending on traffic.

The twins would be busy with after-school commitments until about 8:00 p.m. David had a baseball game and Martha was at a friend's house studying for a history test. That would allow her and Ryan to have a quiet dinner together.

After traveling out of the country and eating airline food, Ryan would appreciate a good home-cooked meal. He loved salmon. Trader Joe's had a fantastic recipe for Mojito Salmon—Wild Pacific Salmon with a Mojito marinade of lime, cilantro, and tomato. She planned to serve the salmon atop brown rice with a spinach salad mixed with walnuts, dried cranberries, and edamame beans.

Ryan took Interstate 405 and Interstate 5 instead of the toll road, hoping to add a few minutes to his trip home. If he arrived too early, it might create some awkward questions. He had told Keri the San Salvador flight would land at LAX at one p.m. She would be expecting him home at about three o'clock—considering the drive to be an hour, plus an additional hour to clear customs, drop his kit bag in flight ops, and get to the employee parking lot,

He was living a lie. The normal excitement of returning home from a trip was replaced with shame. His lies were slowly building a wall between him and Keri—a prison cell of solitary confinement. The more he lied the thicker the wall became. His conscience—the last stopgap between right and wrong—was slowly eroding, lie by lie.

Before his trip to Georgia, he had no proof his *other* life was anything more than a dream, however, that all changed when he met John Dross.

Ryan was certain he had no knowledge of John Dross, Mercy Flight, or the three-story copper fish in front of Atlanta Fish Market except in his *other* life. The only place he could have ever seen or heard of any of them was in the life he lived with Keri after they moved to Georgia from California; the life that was now only a dream.

Keri knew John Dross, but she should have no recollection of the copper fish, just as she had no recollection of having ever moved to Georgia from California.

Tonight he would test her, simply to confirm he was not going crazy and his *other* life did actually exist.

His only knowledge of the big copper fish located in front of Atlanta Fish Market was in his *other* life, when he and Keri lived on Pharr Circle in Buckhead.

Since Keri does not remember having ever lived in the Pharr Circle condo, she should not have any remembrance of the copper fish, as the restaurant moved to Buckhead after Keri moved away.

If asked about the fish, Keri should have no recollection of it or Atlanta Fish Market. This will be one more way to confirm that the only place he could have acquired any memory of seeing the big fish was when he and Keri were living in the condo in Buckhead—in his *other* life.

He pulled into the driveway at 2:40 p.m.—a little earlier than she might have expected.

Keri met him at the door with a kiss and a big hug. "How was San Salvador?"

His head grew hot and his chest tightened at the thought of more lies. "I'm just glad to be home," he said, managing to avoid a lie.

When he reached for his suitcase, he noticed his clothes scattered on the backseat. His heart raced. He had not anticipated Keri meeting him at the car when he arrived home. Keri watched, but said nothing. He ignored the loose clothes, grabbed his suitcase, closed the car door, kissed Keri, and nudged her away from the car.

"Aren't you going to get your clothes out of the backseat?" she said.

He turned and looked, as though he had not noticed them before, and said, "Oh, I'll get those later."

Keri opened the car door. "Nonsense. Here, let me get them." As she retrieved his pants and shirt, she failed to see a business card fall from the shirt pocket onto the garage floor. The card slid under the car.

That was John Dross's business card. That was close.

As they entered the house, the pleasant aroma of a home-cooked meal smacked him in the face, adding thorns to his growing crown of guilt. As she often did on the days he returned from trips, Keri had prepared a special meal for him in an act of love. In return, all he had for her was more lies.

"While you unpack and change, I've got a few last-minute details to take care of in the kitchen. I hope you're hungry. I made one of your favorite meals."

"It smells great! What is it?"

"Mojito Salmon."

Salmon? Again?

"Fantastic!"

Ryan unpacked, showered, and slipped on jeans and a Polo shirt. He remembered John's business card that had fallen from his pocket. Thankfully it slid under his car. If Keri had seen it, he would have been forced to spill the truth; how else could he have explained the card. For now, he was forced to continue living the lie.

After an early dinner, Ryan helped Keri clear the table and clean up the kitchen. "Thank you for an excellent dinner," he said.

"I don't know how you do it."

"What do you mean?"

"Living on airline meals and strange food."

"It's not that bad. However, I do look forward to getting home and eating your cooking. I guess that's what keeps me going."

They moved into the den. "Where are David and Martha?" he said.

"David had a game, and Martha is at a friend's house studying for a test. They should both be home in a couple of hours."

Eager to quiz Keri, he said, "Keri, when was the last time you were in Buckhead?"

"Why do you ask?"

"Just curious."

"Oh, my…I guess the last time I was in Buckhead was in April of 1987 for dad's funeral."

"Have you ever heard of Atlanta Fish Market in Buckhead?"

"No. Why?"

"Are you sure?"

"Positive."

"So you don't remember a restaurant with a statue of a thirty-foot copper fish in front of it?"

"Should I?"

"I guess not."

"Why do you ask?"

I knew it. She's never heard of it.

"The copilot I flew with is from Atlanta," he lied. "During the flight down to San Salvador, we were served fish. We started talking about the best place to eat fish and he mentioned Atlanta Fish Market in Buckhead. I was just wondering if you had ever heard of the place. They relocated to Buckhead in 1993, so I see why you haven't."

"I'm sorry, if I had known you had been eating fish all week, I would've prepared something else for dinner."

"I loved what you prepared tonight. I might've been *served* fish, but that doesn't mean I was *eating* fish. I hardly touched the fish on the plane. Actually, we started talking about good fish restaurants because the fish on the plane was so bad."

"I'm sure Buckhead is not the same place we once knew. We should go back and visit sometime. You can take me to see the big fish."

Now that he knew that Keri had no idea that Atlanta Fish Market existed put him one step closer to solving his dream puzzle. "That sounds like a great idea."

On Monday he planned to call Lewis at the Starbucks in Buckhead to see if the woman named Angela got his note. He would then call John Dross and coordinate a flight to Atlanta for the following weekend of the 26th and 27th. Assuming the woman named Angela was the same woman he knew to be Angel, he would finally learn if she was the key to his life-altering dreams.

The strong sense of déjà vu he experienced during those dreams was too real to ignore and the risk too great to sit around and do nothing. He needed to meet with Angel one last time to ensure that the horror of May 29, 2003, never happens.

CHAPTER 22

Southern California
Easter Sunday morning—April 20, 2003

*R*yan sipped his coffee on the patio, enjoying the stillness of the morning. A hummingbird darted then hovered, probing his needle-like beak deep into a flower searching for nectar.

In years past, instead of a hummingbird, Ryan would have been watching David and Martha dart around in the backyard like explorers searching for treasure.

This was the first year the kids had outgrown hunting for colored, plastic eggs filled with candy and coins. The tradition ended when they were spotted scampering around the yard in their pajamas by classmates eager to spread the word at school. Even Keri's offering to stuff a ten-dollar bill in the golden egg was not enough to tempt them.

Ryan's thoughts drifted to the events of last week. Lewis, at the Buckhead Starbucks, should have given the note to the customer named Angela. He was almost certain that Angela was his Angel. He would call on Monday to get a report.

"Beautiful morning," Keri said.

"Perfect."

Keri sat in the rocker beside him. "I always remember Easter being just like this in Georgia—perfect weather with beautiful new growth on all the trees and flowers. I especially loved the azaleas and dogwoods blooming." She sipped her coffee as she gazed into the yard.

"I was just thinking about all the things I looked forward to as a kid; one of them being Easter, as the official day I was allowed to go barefoot. I also remember my mom wanting to dress me up for church. I hated it."

She turned to him. "I've seen some of those pictures. You looked cute in your little white suit and black and white shoes."

He shot her a disapproving glare followed by a smile. "I'll bet Barbara Ann had fun playing dress up with you, too."

"For her, it was a competition—or a contest among all the mothers who had little girls."

"I'm sure it was."

"I miss the South at this time more than ever; makes me a little bit homesick."

Hearing Keri talk about the South tugged on his heart. During his trip to Georgia, he had similar feelings. The dogwoods and azaleas were in bloom, the people were more engaging and talkative than they were in California; even the familiarly thick air was oddly refreshing—all the things that made him remember "home". He wanted Keri to join him when he returned to Georgia, but she couldn't.

"I guess we'd better start getting ready for church," she said, as she stood. "You know how crowded it is on Easter Sunday."

Ryan turned up his coffee cup, finishing the last cold sip. "Yeah, you're right."

✈ ✈ ✈

Just as Keri had predicted, the church was packed. The added pew takers were mostly out-of-town guests of regular members and twice-a-year attendees—folks who made a special effort to show their spirituality on two days each year—Christmas and Easter.

The congregational singing lasted two songs longer than usual and was followed by a moving offertory solo by Gladys Hooper, *Via Doloroso*.

Ryan expected Pastor Fisher to preach a version of the typical Easter sermon highlighting the miraculous Resurrection of Jesus segued into a message of how Jesus' death was the substitution for the sins of all mankind. A strong close would include a charge to the congregation, urging every person to put their trust in Jesus and receive Him as their personal Lord and Savior, ensuring them of eternal life in Heaven.

As Pastor Fisher moved toward the pulpit, Ryan glanced at the bulletin. The sermon topic read: *Angels in Our Lives*. The word *Angels* piqued his curiosity. He definitely had an Angel in his life—or at least a woman named Angel.

The pastor opened his Bible and laid it on the pulpit. He then stepped away and stood in front of the audience—a rarity, as he never left the safe confines of his large walnut pulpit.

He opened with a question: "Do angels really exist?"

He paused, allowing the crowd to contemplate his question as he paced in front of them. He stopped abruptly and turned toward the blank and befuddled faces.

"If they exist, can you see them? Are angels good or bad? What is their purpose? Are they among us now?"

He spread his arms in the air like a bird. Turning his extended arms into imaginary wings, he flapped them up and down. "Do they have wings?" He moved quickly from left to right on the stage, jumping up and down, while flapping his arms. "Do they fly around us? Are they watching over us?"

Slightly embarrassed for the reverend, Ryan looked to his right at a white-headed woman in her 90s. She appeared somewhere between spellbound and shock, as did much of the audience. Fisher was in uncharted territory. As a meat-and-potatoes preacher, angelology was definitely not on his typical Sunday menu.

After a few passes across the stage, Fisher "flew" back to his pulpit, having gained the attention of every onlooker—especially the biannual attendees.

"The Bible tells us angels do exist," he said, "and yes, sometimes you can see them. There are good angels and bad angels. The good angels are God's messengers on assignments to help people in a variety of ways. Bad angels work for evil purposes trying to tempt people to sin and glorify themselves, not God. The good and bad angels are at war here on earth—fighting for your soul! As far as the wings are concerned, wings are not necessary, and you never know when you might meet an angel, as they mostly appear on earth as humanoids. They are probably among us now—perhaps sitting next to you. Hebrews 13:2 cautions: *Do not forget to show hospitality to strangers, for by so doing some people have shown hospitality to angels without knowing it.*"

At this point, Fisher had the audience sitting on the edge of their seats, looking around, examining strangers for hidden wings or retractable halos.

He continued, "First Timothy 6:16 reveals that humans can't see God directly. But Hebrews 1:14 declares that God sends angels to help people who will one day live with Him in Heaven. Ladies and gentlemen, I ask you…are you one of those people who plan to see God in Heaven? If you are, say amen!"

A weak response drifted from scattered voices among the crowd. "Amen. Amen. Amen."

Fisher pushed the crowd. "I say again! Do you plan to live one day with God Almighty in Heaven? If so, say

AMEN!"

"AMEN!" The audience was coming alive.

"Sometimes the angels among us are invisible, but sometimes they appear in heavenly form, like the angel sitting on the stone of Jesus' tomb after his resurrection, dazzling white, reminiscent of lighting. In Matthew 28:2-4 we read: *After the Sabbath, as the first light of the new week dawned, Mary Magdalene and the other Mary came to keep vigil at the tomb. Suddenly the earth reeled and rocked under their feet as God's angel came down from heaven, came right up to where they were standing. He rolled back the stone and then sat on it. Shafts of lightning blazed from him. His garments shimmered snow-white. The guards at the tomb were scared to death. They were so frightened, they couldn't move.*

"Yes! Angels are real and they are among us now! They are sent by God to Earth as messengers on assignment, answering prayers, giving guidance, and meeting physical needs. God has given angels power that humans don't possess, such as knowledge about everything on Earth, the ability to see the future, and the power to perform work with great strength. But as powerful as they are, angels aren't all-knowing or all-powerful like God.

"While the powerful work of angels may inspire awe, the Bible is clear that we should worship God, not angels. In Revelation, the apostle John began to worship the angel who gave him a vision. In the book of Revelation, the twenty-second book, verses eight and nine, it says: *I, John, saw all these things with my own eyes, heard them with my ears. Immediately when I heard and saw, I fell on my face to worship at the feet of the Angel who laid it all out before me. He objected, "No you don't! I'm a servant just like you and your companions, the prophets, and all who keep the words of this book. Worship God!"* The angels are mighty, yet not Almighty."

Ryan listened intently. His unexplainable dream regressions did not seem so farfetched anymore. Pastor Fisher had offered something much more spectacular than anything that might occur in a dream—angels living among us. If angels are among us, it was completely plausible to him that his dreams could be a venue for the angels to bring him a message. Even if his *other* life was only a dream within a dream, perhaps the angels—who know the future and the past—were trying to teach him something or bring him a message from God.

Angel could very possibly be an angel.

Ryan sensed that Pastor Fisher was reaching the end of his sermon, tying up loose ends and pointing the congregation to the saving work of Jesus Christ on the Cross.

Fisher said, "The Bible records that it was an angel who announced that a miracle happened on the first Easter: Jesus Christ, who had died by crucifixion three days earlier and was buried, rose out of his tomb alive again. Jesus' death was a sacrifice to pay for the sins of fallen humanity to make it possible for them to connect with a holy God. Jesus' resurrection was a miracle meant to give us the real hope that we can have eternal life with God through a personal relationship with His Son, Jesus. AMEN?"

The congregation replied in complete unison, "AMEN!"

Fisher raised his hands high and looked up toward the ceiling of the sanctuary and said, "Imagine the deafening cheers and applause that must have broken out among the angels at the moment of the resurrection. What shouts of glory must have been heard among the cherubim, seraphim, dominions, thrones, powers, and authorities of heaven!"

The organ struck a startling and unexpected chord. The doors to the sanctuary burst open. Men and women dressed in flowing, white robes entered the sanctuary from the rear and marched down the aisles singing *Christ is Risen! Hallelujah*. Everyone stood to their feet. Pastor Fisher was frozen, hands uplifted, singing with the choir. The music director took the stage and urged the congregation to join the choir as they marched onto the platform. Ryan glanced at the little old lady to his right. She was red faced, arms raised, and singing the hymn with all her might.

Once the hymn ended, Pastor Fisher said, "How glorious it is that we serve a risen Savior. The angel said to the women: *Do not be afraid, for I know that you are looking for Jesus, who was crucified. He is not here; he has risen, just as he said.* The angel gives the greatest, most glorious news that the human ear has ever heard: *He is not here; he has risen.* Do I hear an AMEN!"

"AMEN!"

Pastor Fisher said, "Have a wonderful Easter." He turned to the music director and said, "Lead us in a closing chorus."

The music director motioned to the organ, waved his hands at the choir, turned to the congregation and led them in the chorus of *He Lives: "He lives! He lives! Christ Jesus lives today! He walks with me and talks with me along life's narrow way. He lives! He lives! Salvation to impart! You ask me how I know He lives? He lives within my heart."*

Something in the service flipped a switch in Ryan's head. His pursuit of Angel was more personal now than before. After listening to the sermon on angels, he sensed a new dimension to the world around him—a dimension of angelic proportions. Also, the new possibility that the woman named Angel might actually be a real angel in humanoid form sent from God with a message for him.

Tomorrow he would call Lewis at the Starbucks in Buckhead and see if Angela came into the store, and if she might be the woman he was looking for—his Angel.

CHAPTER 23

*R*yan rolled over in bed. The clock on the nightstand glowed 4:10 a.m. Eager to see if Lewis had made contact with Angela, Ryan slipped out of bed, went downstairs, and into the garage—not taking any chances that Keri might hear him making the phone call. Considering the three hour time change, he knew Lewis would be busy making lattes by now. He took extra precaution and sat in the car to place the call.

He dialed the number on Lewis's business card. After the first ring, he put the phone on speaker and adjusted the volume down.

"Starbucks, this is Lewis speaking."

"Hi, Lewis. This is Ryan Mitchell. I was in your store last Thursday and…"

"Yes. I remember. You gave me the note to give to one of my customers."

"That's me. So, did Angela come in over the weekend?"

"Yes."

"Great! Did she say anything after reading the note?"

"I'm sorry, but I have some bad news. I misplaced the note you gave me. I believe one of my employees mistook it for trash and tossed it."

Ryan sank when he heard the news. "Did you happen to mention anything to her about the note...perhaps attempt to describe me to her and see if she remembered ever meeting me?"

"I'm sorry, Mr. Mitchell, but you really didn't tell me too much about yourself. I didn't want to alarm Angela by telling her some man was looking for her."

"I understand. No worries." Ryan paused. Lewis was his only connection to any hope of finding Angel. "Did she come in on both Saturday and Sunday morning?"

"I only saw her on Saturday morning."

Sunday was Easter.

"Listen, thanks for trying. I'll be sure to stop by the next time I'm in your area."

"Again, I'm sorry."

"No problem. Take care."

Ryan sat in the dark car, debating when he should return to Georgia. John had offered to send the Gulfstream over to pick him up whenever he wished—an offer that Ryan still had trouble believing was real. It would have to be a Saturday or Sunday if he wanted to meet Angela. There were two weekends before Mother's Day; the last weekend in April and the first weekend in May. Being gone on Mother's Day would not be the best idea.

He had to fly to Maui on Wednesday and Thursday and was scheduled to be off on the weekend. He either had to drop the Maui trip and tell Keri he was flying on the weekend, or fly the trip and figure out some way to convince her that he had been assigned to fly the weekend, too. Regardless of how he lied to Keri, getting back to Georgia as soon as possible was his top priority.

He dialed John Dross's cell. John picked up on the first

ring. "Hi, Ryan, you need a lift?"

"Wow! I still find this hard to believe."

"Like Mr. Hart said, 'anything'."

"How does Friday sound?"

"The 25th is perfect. I've got a quick trip on Wednesday and Thursday, but I'll be free on Friday. I can be there anytime, but how does ten o'clock Pacific Time sound?"

"That would be fantastic! Unless I hear from you, I'll be at Signature waiting."

"Ryan, I'll take care of your hotel and have a car waiting for you. Is the DoubleTree still good, or would you like a different location?"

"The DoubleTree is perfect."

"I'll take care of it. Look forward to seeing you on Friday at ten o'clock."

"Thank you, John."

If there ever was an angel sent by God to help him, it was John Dross. This was exactly what Pastor Fisher must have been talking about.

If angels are real, what happens to them when their mission is complete? Does the humanoid vanish? Will John Dross vanish after his work is done?

Ryan left the garage and quietly returned to the bedroom. Keri was sound asleep. The digits on the clock read 4:54 a.m. He eased back the covers and slipped into bed.

"Baby," Keri said softly, "where did you go?"

"I couldn't sleep. I went to the kitchen for a snack," he lied...again. Sadly, it was becoming easy.

"Oh," she said.

Her hand rubbed his chest, stomach, and then explored lower. Electric currents shot through his body, arousing him. His heart thumped hard and steady. Her leg slowly crossed over his as she rolled on top of him. Her body was warm and soft. Words were not necessary. They knew each other's thoughts.

As she fulfilled his desires, he could only think of the lies he would have to tell her in the morning.

CHAPTER 24

Southern California
Tuesday noon—April 22, 2003

It was noon before Ryan had the nerve to break the news to Keri he would be out of town on the weekend.

He could easily fly his regularly scheduled trip to Maui on Wednesday and Thursday and be back in plenty of time to meet John on Friday morning at John Wayne Airport. However, that would mean his time at home with Keri before heading to Georgia would be limited.

It was hard enough lying to her, but being gone five days in a row—when he didn't have to—compounded his guilt. His conscious wouldn't let him do it, so he dropped the trip to Maui.

Keri had prepared sandwiches for lunch, but a twisted sick feeling in his gut quenched his appetite when she said, "Don't you have a trip tomorrow?"

"Well, I was supposed to fly tomorrow but crew schedule called and asked if I would fly the same trip on Friday instead."

That's good. Make it sound like it's not your fault.

Keri looked at him with a sad face. "That means you

have to work the entire weekend?"

"I'm afraid so."

"Sunday, too?"

"I'll be home Sunday afternoon." Trying to sound cheerful, he said, "On the positive side, it gives me an extra day of flying, and we could use the money." The sick feeling in his stomach crawled into his chest. She didn't know it, but he was actually losing money by dropping the trip.

"I hate it when you have to work on weekends."

"I know…me, too." He looked at her and faked a smile. "But just think…now I'm off all week."

"I guess so, but it's not the same. You already have to work enough weekends without volunteering for them."

"You're right. I should have said no to crew schedule. That will be the last time, I promise. I'll never do crew scheduling a favor again."

"It's fine. I guess there will be other weekends."

I'm glad that's over.

He put his arm around her shoulder and pulled her tight. "Maybe we can do something special to make up for it."

"What did you have in mind?"

He took her hand. "How about a date…dinner and a movie. You pick the restaurant and the movie."

"Are you saying you'll watch any movie I choose?" She perked up.

"Anything." He had no options.

"Okay, but instead of a dinner date, let's do lunch. Then after lunch come back home and cuddle up and watch my favorite movie of all times, *Gone with the Wind*…beginning to end."

"Sounds great!" he lied. The thought of four hours of Scarlett O'Hara was almost more than he could bear. However, the thought of cuddling up with Keri in the afternoon did sound nice.

"I've got another idea," she said.

"A different movie?"

I shouldn't have said that.

She shot him a questioning look.

"Just kidding," he said.

"Instead of going out for lunch, let's pick something up and bring it back here. That way we will have time to watch the entire movie before David and Martha get out of school."

"Whatever you say. It's your day." Her excitement tempered his guilt. It was the perfect escape.

"So which day do you want to do it? Tomorrow or Thursday?" she said.

"Let's do it tomorrow. Then we can plan something else for Thursday."

"Wow! This is turning out to be much better than a boring weekend. We should do this more often," she said. They laughed.

She was happy. He had done it; his guilt was almost in complete remission. Tomorrow they would get lost in the worries of Scarlett and Rhett and forget about everything else. Watching Atlanta burn would hopefully keep his mind off how badly he would get burned if Keri ever found out about his escapades to Georgia.

CHAPTER 25

Southern California
Wednesday afternoon—April 23, 2003

*R*yan and Keri were comfortably nestled on the sofa. Seeing Keri deeply engrossed in the movie had given him a peaceful satisfaction. However, the whirlwind of drama that resulted mostly from Scarlett O'Hara's wicked attempts at manipulation, deception, and lies, reminded him of his own twisted plans. He was no better than the evil character, Scarlett.

As the final scene played, he saw himself as Scarlett, begging Keri not to leave him after finding out about his trips to Atlanta and numerous lies. "Oh Keri!" Keri walked to the bedroom door. "Keri!" He runs down the stairs after her. "Keri, Keri!" He catches her as she's walking out the front door. "Keri! Keri…if you go, where shall I go, what shall I do? I promise…all of the lies…all of the trips to Atlanta…it was all for us—our future. Please don't leave me. What will I do without you?"

"Frankly my dear, I don't give a damn." Keri walked off into the fog as the orchestral music heightens, bringing the intense drama to a close.

Ryan's heart sank. He was alone...or at least that's the way he imagined it could be if Keri found out what he was doing behind her back. Scarlett simply said she would think about it tomorrow, and closed the door. After shedding a few tears, she remembers Tara and any thought of Rhett is quickly replaced by her love for the red dirt of her homeland. Losing Keri would not be so easy. If Keri left him, he would need more than the red dirt of Georgia to get over her.

"Wasn't that wonderful?" Keri said. "Didn't you just love it?" She snuggled up close and kissed him. "Thank you for a wonderful day—the best ever!"

"I enjoyed every minute," he lied. He was disturbed how easily the lies rolled off his tongue with little restraint.

"How are you going to top that tomorrow?"

"Let me think." He had nothing. He had promised her a second day of escape, but he had no idea what to do. To be honest, if he could leave for Georgia today, he would.

"I know you'll think of something. You are so romantic." She kissed him with passion.

When she pulled back, he said, "We *could* do more of *this* tomorrow."

"Sounds good to me." She kissed him again.

Her affection heaped coals of fiery guilt on his heart.

She pulled him to his back on the sofa and straddled her legs on top of him. "I'm not going to let you leave me like Rhett left Scarlett." Her voice was breathy with a slight quiver. Her eyes were filled with passion.

Right here in the living room at three o'clock in the afternoon?

"What about the kids? Don't we have to pick them up?" he said.

She pulled his T-shirt off. "No. They have stuff to do

after school. They won't be home for hours." She stood up and slipped her shorts off followed by the rest of her clothes. Then, like a magician, she stripped him of his workout shorts and underwear. She grabbed a blanket and returned to her mounted position. Her body was like a furnace. His thoughts were scrambled as his animal instincts took over. For whatever reason, *Gone with the Wind* had triggered her passions. Perhaps it was the thought of Scarlett's constant longing for Ashley, or maybe her secret love for Rhett— possibly the red dirt of Tara.

CHAPTER 26

Southern California
Friday morning—April 25, 2003

*R*yan exited the 73 toll road at MacArthur Boulevard and drove north towards the John Wayne—Orange County Airport. Within minutes, he spotted the Mercy Flight Gulfstream standing tall on the ramp in front of Signature Flight Support.

Waiting at the traffic light on the corner of MacArthur and Campus Drive, he glanced to his left at a Starbucks he had frequented on numerous occasions. He took it as a sign that his trip back to Georgia to the Buckhead to locate Angel was the right thing to do; even though he had lied to Keri, telling her he was instead flying a trip to Maui.

Once he located Angel, he would no longer need to lie. He was absolutely convinced she was his ticket to the most important dream regression of all—the driveway in front of Keri's house, sitting in his 1965 four-door Chevrolet Impala. That was the one place—the only place—in all of time where he would have the chance to change every mistake in his past.

The driver behind him blew the horn. Ryan had not

noticed the light had changed. He turned left on Campus Drive and into the parking lot at Signature. He parked at the far end of the parking lot away from the main entrance.

While sitting in the car, he quickly pulled off his uniform shirt and slipped on a white Polo shirt. He grabbed his roller bag from the backseat, locked the doors, and checked the time—9:50 a.m.

As he approached the lobby door, John was there to greet him. "Good to see you again," John said. They shook hands.

Ryan withheld the urge to thank John, knowing John would only remind him of what Ronald Hart had said about doing *anything*. "Did you have a good flight over?"

"Smooth as glass. It's a beautiful day for flying. I expect the same going back, plus a nice tailwind."

Again, Ryan had to fight the urge to humbly thank John. "I can't wait," Ryan said. It was hard to believe all John was doing. Only a small elite group of humans who populated the social class tagged as the "Rich and Famous" ever experience such treatment. Personal jets to wherever their dreams desired; people dedicated as human shields to absorb the drudgery of life; and never a worry of having enough money to do whatever their minds could imagine.

"We are ready to go when you are," John said.

"I'm ready."

They kept walking through the lobby and exited onto the ramp. The stairs leading up to the cabin of the Gulfstream were lowered. Signature had placed a red carpet at the foot of the stairs. Without breaking stride, John led Ryan up the stairs and into the jet. He took Ryan's roller bag and put it in a closet. "Ryan, you remember my son, Michael?"

"Yes."

Michael turned from the copilot's seat in the cockpit and offered his hand. "Welcome aboard Captain Mitchell."

Ryan shook his hand. "Thank you, Michael."

"Ryan," John said, motioning toward the luxurious cabin of the Gulfstream, "make yourself at home. If you need anything let me know. There's plenty of food in the galley if you get hungry."

"Thank you, John."

John closed the entry door to the jet and joined Michael in the cockpit.

Ryan took a window seat in one of the plush leather executive chairs in the cabin and buckled his seatbelt. Staring out the cabin window, he thought of Keri. He was blessed to have a woman like her as his wife. She adored him. She sacrificed everything to make his life wonderful. Very few men, in their wildest imaginations, would believe there was such a woman anywhere on earth like her. He loved everything about her. She could do no wrong—unlike him.

He hated that he was living a lie and Keri was the victim—the one person in the entire world that he loved the most. But he believed he was doing it for her—for them. If he stretched it, he was not *technically* lying—maybe a little, but for a good cause. He liked to think he was only withholding the truth for a short time until he could make things right. If he was successful in finding Angel, he might never have to tell Keri about anything. He would simply wake up in a new world where all of their mistakes of the past were erased.

After a short taxi, the Gulfstream rolled into position on the runway. The muffled whine of the jet's engines spun up to takeoff power. Ryan gazed out his window as the world zipped by in fast forward. Higher and higher they climbed; objects on Earth growing smaller; the world slowing down. Unable to realize the speed at which they traveled, the jet appeared to be suspended—motionless—floating among the clouds. Frazzled from late nights and worried sleep, Ryan—now relaxed—drifted off to sleep.

His heart filled with a sense of great peace. The air was

fresh with the scent of Spring. The warmth of the sun encouraged thoughts of the beach and the sound of gentle, rhythmic lapping of water against cool, soft sand. Life's worries did not exist in this tranquil place. He was in high school. Keri was there, strikingly beautiful and unknowingly flirtatious. Her smile cast a spell on his heart, holding his eyes captive to her every move. He studied her oval face with alluring brown eyes and butter-soft lips, framed by her shoulder-length chestnut-brown hair.

She took his hand and moved it to her face as though she sensed his desire to touch her. His heart raced; his body tightened. She moved closer; her eyes telling him to kiss her. Their lips touched.

The jet momentarily jolted as it hit rough air. Ryan jumped. His eyes opened.

It was a dream.

He turned and gazed out the window at the earth below. He didn't recognize the terrain or where they might be. He had no idea how long he had been asleep. He checked his watch—11:30 a.m. He breathed deep and exhaled.

Continuing to gaze out the window, he reflected on the pleasant sensation of his dream. He and Keri were young and in love—it was their first love. Their lives had not yet been scarred by regret, pain, and heartache.

I wish I could go back to those days, if only for an hour.

After landing at Peachtree DeKalb Airport, John taxied the Gulfstream to the Mercy Flight hangar. Peering out the cabin window, Ryan noticed dedicated employees standing by, eager to coddle and cosset the jet—tuck it away in the hangar out of the sun where they could return it to an immaculate appearance.

John exited the cockpit. "Your rental car is parked out

front and your room is booked at the DoubleTree. I'm sorry I can't drive you there. I've got some work to do here."

"John, don't worry about me. I know my way around."

"Also, I have a quick trip tomorrow morning down to Dothan, Alabama, but should be back by noon. I'm free if you would like to have dinner tomorrow night."

"That sounds good. I'll look forward to it."

He accepted John's dinner invitation hesitantly. If Angel showed up at the Starbucks on Saturday morning wearing her *Angel* perfume—as he hoped she would—and if the perfume sent him on another dream regression, there were no guarantees that he would wake up in the DoubleTree Hotel in Buckhead, Georgia. He could only assume that John's reality would also shift, making him oblivious to their scheduled dinner meeting.

John took Ryan's roller bag and walked him to the car. "I'll pick you up at six tomorrow night."

"I'll be waiting in the lobby."

Maybe.

CHAPTER 27

Buckhead, Georgia
Saturday morning—April 26, 2003

*T*he alarm clock jolted Ryan from a deep, dreamless sleep. *Hotel...Georgia...Buckhead...Starbucks...Angel.*

He checked the time—4:45 a.m. Starbucks opened at 5:30 a.m.

He flipped on the lamp by his bed. He had plenty of time to shower, shave, dress, and then drive the short distance to Starbucks before they opened. If Angel was true to her schedule, she would be there first thing. He absolutely could not be late.

Ryan parked in the same spot as he had on the morning of his original encounter with Angel. At 5:25 a.m., he watched from his car as employees busily readied the store for customers. He spotted Lewis fiddling with a handful of keys as he walked toward the double doors. Ryan exited his car and arrived at the door just as Lewis was turning the key in the lock.

"Hi, Lewis. Remember me?"

"Absolutely. You're Ryan Mitchell...the guy who left the note for Angela."

"Yep. That's me, and hopefully your 'Angela' will show up this morning."

"She should. She rarely misses coming in early on Saturdays and Sundays. Last weekend was Easter and she might have been out of town visiting relatives."

Ryan loved hearing Lewis's encouraging words. In a matter of minutes, Angel should walk through the door and his search would be over. He might not even need to speak with her, once he took in a deep draw of her perfume. One sneeze and he would be on his way. However, he would like to learn more about this mystery woman before she got away. Who was she? Where did she live? Where does she work? He even considered telling her about his dreams and the part she had played.

Ryan ordered his coffee, took a seat by the door, and checked the time—5:40 a.m. He not only carefully examined customers as they walked through the door, he also scanned the parking lot, making sure Angel did not remain in the car while someone else came in for the beverages. He remembered she drove a big Mercedes, but he couldn't count on her being in the same car since it was one year earlier than when he had originally seen her.

While taking a sip of coffee, he saw a car pull up to the curb with a female driver that looked familiar. The woman drove a boxy-looking Mercedes G-Class SUV instead of the big sedan. When she exited the SUV, he focused hard into the dark morning.

It looks like her!

He stood ready to open the door, ensuring he would get a whiff of her perfume.

✈ ✈ ✈

Captain John Dross wheeled into his reserved parking spot at the Mercy Flight hangar. The air was crisp and the sky was clear over the entire Eastern United States. He whistled a chipper tune as he entered the hangar. The Gulfstream had been towed onto the ramp and Michael was just finishing up the exterior preflight.

John saw his two passengers seated in the lobby. They stood as he approached. "Good morning, Ronald," John said, extending his hand.

"Mornin', Captain John."

While shaking Ronald's hand, John put his left arm around the young lady standing beside Ronald and tucked her in a hug. "How's my little girl doing this morning?"

"Great! How 'bout you, dad?"

"Fantastic! It's a beautiful day to fly…and you know how much I love to fly." Ronald and John's daughter made eye contact and smiled.

"We sure do," a woman's voice said as she joined them.

"Hi, honey," John said, giving the woman a kiss on the lips.

John turned to his daughter. "Susan, did Michael load your bags?"

"Yes, sir."

"Great! So when you guys are ready we can blast off for the Peanut Capitol."

John led the group to the jet and followed them up the stairs into the cabin. He closed the entry door as everyone found a seat. Before going to the cockpit, John addressed the group, "Is everyone comfortable?"

"We're all good, dad," Susan said.

"There's food, juice, and coffee in the galley," John said. "Flying time today is the same as always: twenty-nine minutes once we are airborne."

"Thanks, honey. Now you and Michael fly safe."

"Always, dear," John said.

Ryan Mitchell knew nothing about John's family—yet. John was waiting for the right time to introduce Ryan to his wife, daughter, and son-in-law. John knew they would accept Ryan as family the minute they met him.

John's son-in-law, Ronald, was Philip Darby's only son. Philip Darby had been Ronald Hart's personal lawyer and best friend. Considering the close relationship that John had to both men, it was not a surprise when his daughter, Susan, started dating Philip's son, Ronald. They attended Pace Academy and both graduated from the University of Alabama where Ronald attended law school—as did his father. They were married shortly thereafter. They decided to remain in Alabama and picked Dothan, located in the southeastern corner of the state. Dothan was a friendly community within a short drive of the Gulf Coast. In addition, it had two large hospitals and scads of physicians and clinics. This was a great asset for Ronald's career as he specialized in medical malpractice defense representing doctors, physician groups, and clinics throughout Alabama and Georgia. He was also the chief legal counsel for Mercy Flight, Inc.

Ryan opened the door as the woman approached. She reminded him of Angel in many ways, but it had been too long to be certain. He inhaled deeply several times as the woman entered. "Thank you," she said, giving Ryan a strange look as she noticed his heavy inhalations.

The air was absent any hint of the sweet fragrance.

Walking back to his seat, he noticed Lewis motioning to him. Lewis mouthed silently, "Angela, that's her." Ryan eased over in line behind the woman as though he were waiting for a refill.

If she is wearing the perfume, I missed it.

Standing directly behind her, he leaned his head down slightly and drew in more deep breaths, hoping to catch a scent of perfume. The woman must have noticed. She stepped away, giving him a slight look of disgust. "Is something wrong," she said.

"I'm sorry, but…I thought I knew you."

"So…is that how you tell if you know someone—you smell them?"

"Please forgive me. My name is Ryan Mitchell. Your name wouldn't happen to be Angel, would it?"

"No. My name is Angela."

Ryan knew he was wasting his time. This was not his Angel. Lewis had made a mistake. Talking to her any longer would only make things worse, considering how he had already made a fool of himself with his heavy breathing and sniffing her like a dog from the moment she entered the store.

He made eye contact with Lewis who mouthed, "I'm sorry."

His heart sank, not knowing if the woman named Angel still lived in the area—or even if she existed at all. He would wait a little longer and then try one more time on Sunday morning. If she didn't show up, he would have to call off the hunt. At least he could stop living a lie—a thought that lifted his spirit.

He would give her until 6:30 a.m. before he left. He checked the time—6:15 a.m.

CHAPTER 28

*A*t seven o'clock, after finishing his second cup of coffee, Angel had not shown up. He left Starbucks, hoping tomorrow would be the day he met Angel. If not, the hunt would end.

With little to do, he decided to take a nostalgic drive around Buckhead. When he passed the big, copper fish in front of Atlanta Fish Market, he remembered how hopeful and excited he had been the day he and John ate lunch there.

Even if he never found Angel, his life looked a bit brighter after meeting John and learning of his past association with Keri's father, Ronald Hart. But the thought of telling Keri everything that had happened made his stomach turn. It made him think of the last scene in *Gone with the Wind* as Rhett gave Scarlett his "Frankly my dear..." line and walked off into the fog. He hoped Keri would not do the same to him after she learned of his many lies.

Heading out of Buckhead, he continued driving until he arrived at the little house where he and his mother had lived during his senior year in high school after his father died. The house appeared much smaller than he remembered. Paint was peeling off the sides and the screen door was torn. The swing on the front porch where his mom loved to spend evenings was in need of repair. Slats were missing and one of the chains that held it to the ceiling had broken.

He remembered the day he arrived at the little house after driving from Dallas to pack her belongings and move her to Texas to live with him. He had arrived a day earlier than planned and had caught her by surprise. She had cooked a full-blown Thanksgiving meal—Turkey and all the trimmings—enough food for a family of six. The next morning she fed him one of her famous big breakfasts like she did when he was in high school: grits, bacon, eggs, and home-made biscuits with his favorite Mayhaw jelly.

There was no sign of anyone living in the house. He pulled the car into the driveway. Gravel crunched under the tires as he rolled slowly to a stop. He exited the car and walked to the front porch. He pulled open the screen door and peered into the house through a pane of glass. The house was empty. He twisted the door knob, finding it unlocked and stepped inside. The air was stale with a hint of something rank—possibly a dead rodent or bird.

The house was tiny—a den with a door leading into the kitchen; a hallway that led to two bedrooms in the back of the house, each with their own small bath. He walked through the house, the wooden floor creaking with every step. Sadness filled his heart as he thought of his dear mother living in such a rundown hovel—though she never complained, always seeing the best in life regardless of her circumstances. She would often say that she was just passing through this life and on her way to her real home in Heaven.

He left the house and sat in his car reflecting. His mother was in her real home, no longer chained to this broken world. No more broken swings and screen doors to repair. No more peeling paint to worry about. No more sick body and mind.

She was finally free. His eyes became watery and his chest tightened. He missed her. "I love you mom."

He started the car and backed out of the driveway.

The Gulfstream touched down at the Dothan Regional Airport exactly twenty-nine minutes after takeoff from Peachtree DeKalb Airport. John taxied to Aero-One Aviation where ramp attendants stood ready to service the jet and assist Michael with the luggage.

Standing at the bottom of the stairs on the ramp, John said, "I hope you guys have a great time."

"I wish you and Michael could stay with us...if only for the weekend," Susan said.

"Me, too, but we've got to fly a trip to California tomorrow." John walked with them to the lobby.

He hugged Susan, shook Ronald's hand followed by a man hug and a pat on the back, and kissed his wife. "I'll check my schedule for next weekend, but I should be able to fly down and pick you up on either Saturday or Sunday. If not, I'm sure the children won't mind keeping you a couple of extra days."

"Not at all," Ronald said. "We love having her and she can stay as long as she likes."

"Dad, remember, we want you and mom to come down and spend Mother's Day with us, or we can come up and be with you guys...either way."

"Let's see...Mother's Day is weekend after next, right?"

"Yes," Susan said. "Sunday, May 11th."

"I'll pencil that in."

"Dad, I think you better use ink on that one."

John chuckled. "Don't worry sweetheart, unless the good Lord has other plans, we will definitely be together on Mother's Day."

"Oh, dad! I almost forgot. Ronald will be out of town the entire first week of June, and I wanted me, you, mom, and Michael to spend that week at the beach together."

"That sounds fantastic! I could use some time off, and I don't think Michael will object." John turned to Ronald. "Sorry you can't be with us."

"John, you need to be with your family and this is the perfect time to go to the beach. I'll catch you on the next trip," Ronald said.

"Okay...so I'll work on something for Mother's Day weekend and plan to be off the entire first week of June."

"Perfect," Susan said.

"I'd better get going." John hugged Susan once more, and then kissed his wife.

"See you next weekend," Susan said.

"Take care of my Angel. God only made one."

"Don't worry dad, she's our Angel, too."

John turned and walked away.

CHAPTER 29

Buckhead, Georgia
Saturday afternoon—April 26, 2003

When Ryan arrived back at the hotel, he was exhausted. His eyes burned and his body felt like concrete. He dropped on the unmade bed, thinking a short nap would pep him up and keep him from being a listless zombie at dinner with John. He kicked his shoes off and closed his eyes. He dreamed…

"Sounds like you need one of your momma's hot biscuits and some Mayhaw jelly," his mom said, placing a plate of steaming biscuits on the table. "That ought to fix you right up."

I'm with my mother…in our old house.

"So, how did your date go last night? I'll bet it was hard for you to say good-bye to my sweet little Keri."

It's not right! This is not the right dream! I should be with Keri…at her house…in the car. I have to stop her from breaking up with me!

"Mom! Listen to me! Keri just dumped me and I need to fix it! Do you understand? I must go talk to her and get her to change her mind!"

"Ryan, calm down. Everything is going to be just fine." She poured a cup of coffee and took a seat. She fiddled with a tiny cross hanging from a thin, silver chain around her neck.

"I'm not hungry. I need to go see Keri before it's too late."

"What you need is a good breakfast. We can talk about it while you eat. Keri isn't going anywhere."

He reluctantly took a seat and started to eat. Even in his dream he could smell the biscuits and taste his favorite Mayhaw jelly. His worries about Keri seemed to be pushed aside for the moment.

She took a sip of coffee. "Give her some time. We both know how this turns out, don't we? Not even Barbara Ann was able to stop it." She handed him a napkin from the stack in the plastic holder on the table.

Ryan stopped eating and gazed at his mother. "How do you know how it turned out? You're dead."

"We knew all along you two would get together. But I must admit, I had hoped it would not be so messy...you know...all the detours down misery lane...with Rex and that little tramp, Emily Anderson. Son, I tried to warn you about women like that, but you didn't listen."

"You know about that, too?"

"Yes, Ryan, we know about everything. If you had only listened to your mother, you could have saved yourself from most of the pain you went through. But you had to learn the hard way...most people do."

He couldn't explain it, but he was having a conversation with his dead mother in a dream, talking about things that only he knew about.

"Okay, you were right," he said. "But as you now know,

Keri and I did finally get together. Everything turned out fine."

"Yes, but think what it *could* have been like if you had never met that little floozy on the beach or that disgusting friend of yours; I thought I taught you better. Because of your bad decisions, my poor little Keri got pushed aside and suckered into Rex's trap." She took a sip of coffee. "I do wish all that could have been avoided, but once it's done, it's done. There's no going back. So, please, do your momma a favor and try not to make anymore foolish choices."

"I fixed all that. It never happened. Remember back when I was still in the Navy and I called you from California on your birthday, and you gave me Keri's address?"

"Yes, that was sweet. You always called me to wish me a happy birthday."

"Well, I had a strange dream and was able to live that day over again. I made different choices. When I woke up from the dream, Keri had never married Rex and I never married Emily."

"I know all that," she said. "But in your *other* life, you still married Emily. So although you think you fixed everything, you will live with the reminder of what could have happened, which is not a bad thing. Maybe now you will respect those ugly life-altering consequences that result from bad choices."

"Why doesn't Keri remember?"

"It was your dream and your life, not Keri's. When you changed things, Keri never had to experience the ugly consequences of your previous choices. Keri was always supposed to be in your life, but your bad choices delayed it. As you know now, because you didn't go to the condo in New York, Keri didn't get pregnant with David. And by not going with Rex to the beach, you escaped Emily's trap and avoided being seduced into marrying her, and Keri never married that jerk, Rex Dean. As a result, you and Keri married years earlier."

He let what she was saying soak in. She was right. His choices had not only affected *his* life, but the lives of those around him.

He said, "Well, in our situation, it was mostly Rex's fault. He's the one that kept us apart when he changed the letters."

"Is that what you learned from your dream?"

"What do you mean?"

"You're trying to shift the blame away from yourself. It's not about Rex, it's all about you. You can always find a 'Rex' to blame, but in the end, you—not Rex—must live with the consequences. By the way...you and Keri would have figured out the letters if you had not gone to the beach with Rex."

"What makes you so sure?"

"Trust me, I just know."

"You sure do claim to know a lot to be dead."

"Listen, you are not the first, nor will you be the last, to make a bad decision. People have been making bad choices since the beginning of time, and they all have ugly consequences—some life-altering. Take Adam and Eve for example; they are the 'poster children' for bad choices. You might even say it was their choice in the Garden of Eden that birthed *every* bad choice since then. You followed Rex to the beach just as Eve listen to Satan—her 'Rex'—and pulled the fruit from the forbidden tree in the Garden of Eden and did eat. Emily was your forbidden fruit. Your dream was given to you to show you that you had a choice; we always do. We were sitting right here in this house when I told you that if you were not careful your heart would deceive you."

"I know! I know! I was a stupid kid back then."

"Hopefully you're a little wiser now." She fingered the cross again. "I'll tell you what you need to do."

"What?"

"After you finish your breakfast, you need to take a shower, get dressed, and go back over to Keri's house. You need to tell her that your life will never be right without her, and you are willing to do whatever it takes to make sure you don't lose her. I see great things in your future."

"But I'm leaving this afternoon for the Academy, and she will be at church. I'll miss her."

His mother ignored his comment.

He begged, "Help me. I don't know what to do?"

She just sat there, holding her little cross, running it back and forth on the thin, silver chain around her neck. "Ryan, life is a test without a time limit. Just as I tried to tell you when you were a young man, you have a great opportunity ahead. Whether you seize it or not will depend on a very important principle."

"I'm all ears. I'm listening this time. Tell me what to do and I'll do it!"

He sensed the seriousness in her pause. She looked deep into his soul filling him with a peace that was not of this world.

She said, "Ryan, have mercy on others, be compassionate, and serve them. Put others before yourself—starting with your wife and family. The poor in spirit, and those who mourn, are the ones who are conscious of their own selfishness. Because of this they are meek and merciful in their attitudes and actions toward others. The greatest blessings in life flow into the lives of those who show mercy to others."

Her words were not from his mother but from some other place—a place beyond his dream.

"I understand! I know I failed and made many mistakes. Can you help me? If I could go back and do it all over again, I would definitely do things differently. How can I get her back? What can I say? I'm leaving this afternoon."

She said, "God put you and Keri on this earth and

designed each of you for a specific purpose. If you want to be truly happy and fulfilled, learn to serve others—start with your wife."

But this is a dream. Keri and I are together. Our lives are half over. What am I thinking?

"Don't worry about that!" Martha said.

"About what?"

"What you were thinking."

"How did you know what I was thinking? How did you do that?"

"Forget how I do what I do. Trust me. It will all work out if you follow my advice. Don't let her get away this time. You two were meant to be together from the beginning. You can change *everything* if you act now. Have faith and don't worry about the Academy."

He pushed back from the table. "Should I go to her house now?"

His mother had mysteriously disappeared. He was alone in the little kitchen.

"Knock! Knock! Knock!" Ryan jumped.

Did I oversleep? Oh no! John!

"Excuse me! Housekeeping!" The door clicked open and a woman walked in the room.

"Would you like your room cleaned?" the woman said.

Sitting up on the bed, he said, "No, it's fine. Just leave me some fresh towels and wash cloths. That should be fine." The maid worked quickly and was gone in three minutes. He checked the time—3:25 p.m. He had slept for two hours.

He sat staring out the window. "I just had a conversation with my dead mother. How weird was that? She had a clear mind—free from Alzheimer's—and she knew everything, even what happened to me after she died."

How was that possible?

He must have been projecting his thoughts into his dream mother. That's how she knew what he was thinking. Everything she said must have been what he wanted her to say.

Then it suddenly hit him that in the dream his mother had referred to "we" when he first asked how she knew everything that had happened. She had said, "*We* knew all along you two would get together." And "...*we* know about everything." Who was "we"?

Perhaps she was referring to her and God? But what about Angel, how does she fit into all this? I wonder if mom knows Angel. Maybe God and mom are working together and they sent Angel to Earth to straighten things out...like Pastor Fisher said.

He smiled.

Those were not my thoughts.

CHAPTER 30

Buckhead, Georgia
Saturday evening—April 26, 2003

After a good workout in the hotel gym, followed by a shower, Ryan waited in the lobby of the DoubleTree at 5:55 p.m.—starving.

John had not mentioned where he planned to go for dinner, but Ryan hoped he might suggest they return to the Atlanta Fish Market. Their lunch the previous week was amazing. There were several selections on the menu he would love to try.

The black Lexus pulled up at exactly six o'clock. After Ryan was in the car, John said, "It's up to you, but would you like to go back to Atlanta Fish Market?"

"You must be a mind reader. That sounds great."

"From the way it looked at lunch last week, I thought you might like to give it another try."

When they arrived at the restaurant, the hostess said, "Right this way, Mr. Dross."

He never gave the hostess his name. He must be a regular.

When Ryan opened his menu and began processing the

selections, his mouth started to water.

TODAY'S FRESH CATCH
Select Your Fish – Select Your Preparation

New Zealand King Salmon, GA Mountain Rainbow Trout, Atlantic Mahi Mahi, Nova Scotia Halibut, Block Island Swordfish, Atlantic Red Snapper, and more—sautéed, broiled, blackened or Hong Kong Style.

He scanned the ENTRÉE SPECIALTIES: *Sizzling Whole Red Fish, Swordfish "Cashew & Cracked Pepper Crusted", Mahi Mahi Teriyaki, Cedar Planked Short Smoked Atlantic Salmon*, and more.

"Do you see anything that strikes your fancy," John said.

"All of it!"

John chuckled. "You can't go wrong with any of it."

"That's my problem. I'm starved and I could literally eat some of everything. It's going to be tough just selecting one." His eyes drifted over to the APPETIZER SPECIALTIES and SOUPS, SALADS.

John said, "Take your time, but I think I'm going to have the *'Pecan Crusted' Salmon Trout Filet with Bourbon Honey Butter, Whipped Sweet Potato and Broccoli*."

"That sounds tempting." Ryan narrowed it down to two possible selections. "Let me see…I had the salmon last week, so I think I'll go with the *Swordfish 'Cashew & Cracked Pepper Crusted'*."

"Sounds great, and I think you'll love that side of cheesy grits that comes with it."

"My mom made the best cheese grits I've ever put in my mouth. I can't wait to try these."

"I'll bet Martha was a fantastic cook," John said.

"Did you know my mom?"

"Not formally, but I remember Keri talking a lot about her. Keri and your mom must have been close."

"Very close." Ryan took a sip of water. "So, how did your trip to Dothan go this morning?"

"Perfect. My wife is spending the week there,"

Surprised, Ryan said, "You never told me you were married."

"I had hoped to introduce you to my family this weekend, but they had already made plans to go to Dothan."

"Why Dothan?"

"My daughter, Susan, and her husband, Ronald, live in Dothan. Since I planned to be out of town most of next week, my wife thought it would be a good time to visit."

"That sounds nice. Do you get to spend much time with them?"

"They come up and visit almost every weekend. My son-in-law handles all of the legal issues for Mercy."

"A lawyer…that's nice."

"His practice is in Dothan where he specializes as a medical malpractice defense lawyer. He is a great asset to Mercy Flight, Inc. taking care of all our physicians."

"That works out nice."

"Do you remember Ronald Hart's lawyer, Philip Darby?"

"Sure. Wonderful man. He coordinated Mr. Hart's final arrangements with us."

"My daughter married Philip's son."

"Wow! One big happy family."

"Yeah…we are blessed. Philip actually named his son, Ronald, after Mr. Hart."

"From what I remember, Mr. Hart and Mr. Darby were good friends."

"Yes, they were like brothers."

"Are there any grandchildren?"

"Not yet. Susan is a CPA and oversees the financial side of the Mercy operation. She stays fairly busy."

What a nice package. John's son is being groomed for

the chief pilot job, John's daughter handles the money, and the son-in-law is the chief counsel. Ryan couldn't wait to find out more about John's wife. She was probably Darby's sister or possibly a cousin of Mr. Hart's.

The conversation stopped when the server brought their meals. "This looks fantastic!" Ryan said.

"I hope you enjoy it," the server said.

John and Ryan were quiet for the next five minutes as they enjoyed the first samples of their fish dinners. Each bite brought audible confirmations of enjoyment. The only words spoken between bites were words describing how tasty the food was.

"Ryan," John said, "you and Keri should come over and spend the weekend with us. We have plenty of room. It would give you a chance to get to know the family."

"That sounds nice. I'll run it by Keri and see what she thinks. Having fifteen-year-old twins keeps her busy, but maybe we can find a free weekend."

"Bring the kids, too. Like I said, we have plenty of room."

"I'll talk to Keri when I get home and see what we can work out."

The way things were going, this might be his last trip to Georgia—that is…if he didn't see Angel at Starbucks in the morning. If Angel didn't show up, he would have a lot of explaining to do before he could introduce Keri to the Dross family. On second thought, she probably already knew John's daughter, son, and wife. He wouldn't be surprised if she knew Ronald Darby, too.

I'm surprised Mr. Hart didn't match Keri up with Darby's son when they were toddlers.

Keri's dad had surrounded himself with a select group of people that he trusted—people that he knew would carry on the work of Mercy Flight—something he was obviously passionate about.

In his dream, Ryan's mother instructed him to put others first. Chills swept over his entire body. His mind could not process fast enough. He reflected on how kind and serving John had been to him since they first spoke on the phone. John was a living example of what his mother had told *him* to be: selfless, putting others first, compassionate.

And then there was Mercy Flight, Inc. Ryan's mother could have written the company mission statement: *Serving others while being especially merciful to the sick and needy.* Mr. Hart was indeed a saint.

Had he missed his purpose in life? Is it possible Ronald Hart would have taken him under his wing and made him the chief pilot of Mercy Flight, Incorporated? Could he be living John Dross's life?

John said, "Ryan, what are your plans for the next few of months? I want to be available if you need me, but I have a couple of family trips I'm trying to schedule."

"John, you should take care of your family first. You need to spend time with them when you can. Don't worry about me."

John pulled a datebook from his back pocket. "The family always spends holidays together. The next two on the calendar are Mother's Day on Sunday, May 11th, and Father's Day on June 15th. We'll either spend those days in Buckhead or Dothan. And then they wanted me to take the entire first week of June off...that would be the first through the eighth...for a family trip to the Gulf Coast."

This guy is amazing. I can't believe he is so concerned about me.

"That sounds great. Do it!"

"I just wanted you to know the dates I would not be available. However, if you need to go anywhere, I'll have one of our other planes dispatched to take care of you."

"I'll be fine, John. Your family comes first." For the first time, Ryan started seeing things differently. Up until now he had soaked up all the attention and enjoyed it. It felt good to be pampered and served. He remembered his dream mother's words: *You will never find true happiness when you seek to serve yourself. If you want to be truly happy and fulfilled, learn to serve others…*

"Seriously," John said, "I want you to talk to Keri and see if we can work something out for you to come over and visit. It would give me great pleasure to fly over and pick you guys up and show you a wonderful time in Atlanta. The children will love the Georgia Aquarium, the World of Coca-Cola, the Zoo, the Children's Museum of Atlanta, and I know Keri will love shopping and visiting with Mercy. Let's see if we can put something on the schedule before I take off the end of May."

"Did you say 'Mercy'?"

"Yes. That's my wife's name."

"I didn't remember you mentioning her name."

"I probably didn't. If I had, I might have called her Angel."

"Angel?"

This is crazy! He calls his wife Angel?

"Her name is Mercy, but I have almost always called her Angel. I see her as the angel God sent to me. I don't know what I would do without her."

"I like it. I can't wait to meet her."

"You'll love her. I always like to say when I refer to her: God only made one. She's special."

"Just out of curiosity, your wife's name didn't have anything to do with the naming of Mercy Flight, did it?"

"It did…but that was not my doing. Mr. Hart named the company."

"How did that happen?"

"Mercy was Mr. Hart's personal nurse while he was in and out of the hospital with his heart condition." John paused and smiled. "Actually, Mr. Hart first introduced me to

Mercy."

"Seems like he is quite the matchmaker."

John smiled. "I would say we both married *up*, thanks to Mr. Hart."

"Definitely," Ryan agreed.

"So…back to your question. Knowing his life would probably be cut short, he had the epiphany to start up a non-profit to serve the sick and needy and he wanted to name the company after my wife. He said he had never met a person who lived such a caring, selfless, existence. I can vouch for Mr. Hart's observation about my wife. Her name is definitely befitting of who she is in every way."

"She sounds like an amazing woman. I'll talk with Keri first thing when I get home and see when would be a good time to come over and visit," he lied. He was not about to talk to Keri about coming to Georgia.

This is getting messy. I really need to find Angel and let her zap me out of here and into another world—fast!

CHAPTER 31

Buckhead, Georgia
Sunday morning—April 27, 2003

*R*yan parked in front of the Buckhead Starbucks on Peachtree at 4:45 a.m. The store didn't open until 5:30 a.m., but it was his last chance to find Angel, and he couldn't afford to miss her.

After waiting forty-five minutes, Lewis finally unlocked the doors. He greeted Ryan with meaningless chit chat— mostly apologies about his customer, Angela, not being the woman Ryan was looking for. He ordered his coffee, and took it to a table by the front door.

The first few sips of coffee revived him from a sleepless, dreamless, tormented night. He waited patiently, checking each customer that entered the store, hoping his memory would not fail him when his Angel arrived. The more women he saw walk into the store, the more confused he became.

At this point, I probably couldn't pick the woman out of a police lineup. It's been too long.

By seven o'clock he had not seen—or smelled—anyone that reminded him of his Angel. Defeated and hopeless, he left the store. He sat in his car another fifteen minutes hoping for a miracle.

Nothing.

His greatest concern—after all the lies—was facing Keri.

Maybe I shouldn't tell her. Just forget it ever happened. She'll never know.

If he didn't tell her, they would never be able to take advantage of the wonderful benefits that Ronald Hart had intended for them to enjoy. In addition, Ryan would have to constantly be on guard that Keri never spoke with John Dross. Basically, if he didn't come clean and tell her everything, he would be forced to live a lie for the rest of his life—a heavy burden to carry.

I have to tell her...everything!

As painful as he knew telling her would be, he loved her too much not to.

Having accepted that Angel was not going to show, he started the car and returned to the DoubleTree. Up until now, a small part of him believed he would never see John again—at least not in this reality. He was wrong.

John and Michael planned to attend church, but would be at the airport by one o'clock. They invited Ryan to join them at church, but he turned down the offer, not knowing how long he would be at Starbucks.

Packing his suitcase, he wondered what he was going to do for the next four hours. He saw his bottle of *Angel* perfume and considered squirting some on his arm and taking a deep breath—seeing where he might land. But instead of playing a lethal game of Russian Roulette, he tossed it in the trashcan by the dresser.

I'll never need that again.

His eyes were heavy and his body begged for a nap. He put the DO NOT DISTURB sign on the outside of the door and secured the safety latch. After slipping into his boxers, he settled in for a nap.

What the heck! Why not? What have I got to lose?

He popped out of bed, pulled the *Angel* from the trashcan, and pumped a couple of sprays on his arm and around the room. He inhaled several times ingesting the fragrance deep into his lungs.

"Ahhhhh...choooo!!"

There's no turning back now.

He let the reaction take full effect—sneezing, burning eyes, his nose running like a faucet. After fifteen or twenty minutes of torture, he went into the bathroom and blew his nose, washed his face, and returned to the bedroom. He lay perfectly still on the bed with his eyes closed and waited for sleep. After his adrenal juices receded, he calmed. The heaviness of sleep soon followed.

Under a canopy of clear, blue sky, peaceful winds whispered through the branches of easterly bent pines.

Ryan recognized the place to be a cemetery. Grave markers, glistening in the sun, dotted the carpet of rolling green lawns beneath towering oaks and magnolias. The tranquil and somber setting was the shrine of thousands of lost—and often forgotten—loved ones. The world outside had quickly forgotten, but within the boundaries of the cemetery, death, ironically, didn't seem so final.

I'm dreaming. Why am I here?

Ryan watched as his dream doubled leaned down and placed fresh-cut flowers in the floral cone at the foot of a headstone. Like flowers on a dead man's porch, it was a useless act of kindness, as their bones would offer no thanks and the flowers would soon wilt without care. There were three evenly-spaced, granite markers, set flush with the grass—not two.

He read the names and the dates

KERI H. MITCHELL: JUNE 5, 1957 – MAY 29, 2003
DAVID R. MITCHELL: AUGUST 31, 1988 – MAY 29, 2003
MARTHA K. MITCHELL: AUGUST 31, 1988 – MAY 29, 2003

I don't understand!

A crow cawed—a possible trigger—propelling him through an imaginary portal; a crack in time.

The vivid details of May 29, 2003, replayed in his mind with the clarity of the present: the call on his cell phone while driving in darkness to LAX to fly his trip to JFK; the panicked, helpless feeling that nearly sucked the life out of his lungs; the evil in the man's voice that made him choose between his life and the lives of his wife and children; his constant prayers for a miracle that would save his family from the jaws of death—a miracle that never came. Instead, he found their bodies strapped to gurneys in the living room of his house, pumped full of lethal drugs.

Lucid but confused, he struggled to free himself from the horror that engulfed him.

Stop dreaming! Wake up! This isn't real!

His mental cries went unanswered, much like a surgery patient, paralyzed by muscle relaxants, wakes during surgery finding it impossible to move, speak, or make others aware of his distress. It was unlike his other dreams, where he had freely willed himself from room to room and conversed with dream characters as he wished.

"They're gone," a voice said from behind him.

He turned, seeing a woman with a concerned look of empathy observing his grief. "Who are you?" he said.

"Ryan, don't you recognize me? I'm Angel."

"Why are you here? Better yet, why am I here?"

"Just like in all of your dreams, you are here to learn a lesson about change."

"I don't want change! I want things the way they were—

I want Keri back!"

"Ryan, you are not being honest with yourself. You do want change. If not, why do you keep looking for me? I'll tell you why...because you want to change your past. You want to make your life better. But I'm not the one who is going to change things, and contrary to what you think, it's not in your dreams where things are changed. Dreams are worthless unless you wake up and actually act on them. You're not going to change your life until you *choose* to change. It's not about the past, it's about the present, and you are stuck because you haven't learned how to let go of the past. You can only learn from the past, holding on to it will rob you of your hope in the future."

"What about all the things that were beyond my control...like my dad dying and leaving me and my mom broke, or Rex ruining my life when he changed those letters and mailed them to Keri. Those are things that I had no control over. Those are things I can *never* change."

"Yes, some things are out of your control. Your dad died early because he failed to take better care of himself. That was out of your control. But you were responsible for the decisions you made after his death, things you might not have had to deal with if he had lived longer—like caring for your mother. As far as Rex is concerned, you chose Rex as a friend. You chose to live with Rex when you were assigned as an instructor at Top Gun school. The letters would have never been tampered with if you had not been living with Rex. The same goes for the decision you made in New York to accompany Keri to her father's condo. Bottom line...it's not about what happens to you as a result of things that are out of your control—like your father's death—but about the choices you make concerning the things that are within your control—like choosing your friends."

Her words dug deep into his heart. She was right. If he had not been sucked into living with Rex, he and Keri would have reconnected much earlier.

"Life is like a hand of poker. You have to play the hand you're dealt, but in your hand is one very valuable wild card. It lets you change the suit or number on any card. That wild card is called choice. Humans are the only creatures that are able to make moral choices. It is your greatest blessing and can be your greatest curse. As you have proven with your life, people don't always make good choices."

"If it's my lesson, why must my family die?"

"When you wander from the path you were meant to travel, others will suffer. Your life is not just about you."

"So you are telling me I am doomed to a life of suffering and pain as a result of my bad choices...*and* because of the things I cannot even control? That's not fair."

"Very few lessons are learned outside of suffering. Suffering and pain open our ears to hear God. There can be no growth in your life without change...there is no change without loss...and there is no loss without pain. Better choices are the key to avoiding *unnecessary* suffering in your life. You should have learned that by now in your previous dreams."

"Tell me what I could have done to stop this?" He pointed to the grave markers of his family.

"In your first dream, you chose not to go to the condo in New York. That choice stopped the illegitimate birth of your son, David."

"Look!" Ryan snapped back, pointing to the graves. "My family is dead! Who cares about what I did or didn't do in New York?"

Angel continued calmly. "In your second dream, you chose not to go with Rex Dean to the beach, and you guarded the letter you had written to Keri, mailing it yourself."

"What is wrong with you? Again, they are dead. None of

my choices stopped it!"

They can't really be dead because I'm dreaming.

She continued, "And then there was the third dream…"

He snapped, "The third, the fourth, the fifth, and now the sixth…and as far as I know 1,000 more! Who CARES!? My family is still dead! How long is this going to go on?"

"If it helps, I can tell you that the Number Seven is the number of completion, the end, the fulfillment. Seven represents perfection."

"What are you saying?" He took a calming breath. "Just tell me…will I be able to fix this in the next dream?"

"All I can say is that the lessons will continue until the lessons are learned. Your lesson is about making good choices. Life is a choice, and in the end your life will have become the summation of those choices."

"What if I *never* learn what I'm supposed to learn?"

"The journey of life is all about the ending. Each choice is merely another piece added to your personal jigsaw puzzle. In the end, once all the pieces have been connected, you will see the completed picture of your life—good or bad."

Ryan turned and gazed at the grave markers. In a somber tone, he said, "Will I ever see my family again?"

"I'm sorry, but some choices have irreversible consequences. All we can do is learn from the past, embrace the present—don't take anything for granted—and hope in the future."

That's what mom always said.

"Wait! What did you just say? Where did you get that?"

"I'm not sure I know what you are asking."

"What you just said about past, present, and future…"

Could this be the woman mom was referring to in the dream when she said "we"?

"…have you ever known a woman named Martha Mitchell, by chance?"

Angel smiled. "Do you mean your mother, Martha?"

"Yes."

"Martha and I have become very close."

"How is that possible? Were y'all friends before she died?"

Angel pursed her lips. "Not exactly."

"Wait! You said 'have become'? What's that supposed to mean?"

"Well…we met *after* she died."

"After? That's impossible. Wait! Are you telling me you met my mother in Heaven?"

"Yes."

"Are you telling me that you are dead?"

"Not exactly."

"If you are not dead, and you didn't know my mom when she was alive, but you have become very close to her *since* she died…"

"Ryan, I'm an angel. I was sent to guide you."

I'm dreaming. This is completely normal. None of this is real.

"So you are an angel named Angel, and your favorite perfume is Angel." He laughed.

Ryan opened his eyes. He looked around the room. Nothing had changed. He was still in the DoubleTree. His suitcase was on the floor as he'd left it before he went to sleep—packed and ready. He smiled.

He breathed a sigh of relief. Keri, David, and Martha were still alive.

CHAPTER 32

Buckhead, Georgia
Sunday morning—June 8, 2003

Ryan took a long, hot shower after working out in the hotel gym. The therapeutically-charged hot water poured over his body while his mind drifted freely in thought.

He missed Keri. His sensation of loneliness overwhelmed him—stronger than ever before. The visual image from his dream of her name etched in the grave marker haunted him. Although only a dream, his mind toyed with his emotions, twisting the illusion into reality. How could he live without her? She anchored his life, and was emotionally—by far—the stronger of the two of them. If he died first—as he hoped he would—he knew she would be fine. After a short period of grief, she would bounce back, making the most of every day, pouring her life into those around her.

He toweled off, dressed, and left the room. He checked out of the hotel at noon. He went to his rental car, tossed his suitcase in the backseat, and started for Peachtree DeKalb Airport to meet John.

More despairing thoughts dug into his core. Telling Keri the truth about everything that had happened during the last two weeks—all the lies and deception—dumped waves of guilt and remorse on his heart, but he had no other choice.

Why did I do it? Why couldn't I have just left things alone?

As he neared the airport, the sick feeling in his gut verged on nausea. It was 12:50 p.m. local time—three hours earlier in California. He mentally calculated when he would be face-to-face with Keri—approximately three o'clock West Coast time.

His mind spun in a different direction when an oncoming four-door Mercedes sedan streaked past. His instincts collected the image of the car and the driver during the few seconds it was in view, processing it faster than a powerful computer equipped with facial recognition technology. His heart raced. The woman was a near perfect match to his Angel, and the car was identical to the car she had been driving one year in the future when they met at Starbucks.

Is it possible? If so, what would she be doing at Peachtree DeKalb?

He didn't have time to chase after her. If he did, he would be late for his agreed-to departure time with John. He knew John wouldn't mind, but it would add to his and Michael's day, as they planned to fly back to Atlanta after dropping him in California. More than likely, his mind was playing tricks on him—again. He so desperately wanted to find his Angel that the slightest common feature of almost any woman might cause him to think it was her.

He parked the rental next to John's black Lexus SUV and went inside the hangar. The Gulfstream had been pulled onto the ramp and looked ready.

John greeted him with a handshake. "We're ready to go when you are," John said, offering to take his bag.

"Thanks, but I'll take it."

Something about John looked different—his nose as red as Rudolf, his cheeks glowing.

Ouch!

"Looks like you got a little sun," Ryan said.

"Yeah. I should have used more sunscreen. But I figure the vitamin D will do me good...as long as my skin holds up." He laughed.

Ryan was confused as to how John might have gotten sunburned at church. The burn, much worse than anything possible from merely sitting in the morning sun on his patio for an hour, looked deep, as though he had spent several days on the beach. Unable to make any sense of it, he released the thought.

With John leading the way, they continued to the jet. After boarding, Ryan spoke briefly with Michael, noticing he, too, looked slightly sunburned on his ears and nose.

Ryan took a seat in the cabin. John joined Michael in the cockpit and had the jet airborne within fifteen minutes, headed for California.

During the flight, Ryan nodded off a couple of times and snacked on a fruit and cheese platter John had catered for the trip. He spent practically every waking moment perplexed about facing Keri with the truth.

When he wasn't spinning scenarios in his mind about Keri's possible reactions to his confession, he dealt with the unexplainable loneliness that hung over him like a suffocating illness.

He had no reason to entertain such thoughts of loneliness, other than the lingering memory of his dream. The dates of death on the markers were May 29, 2003—the same date when Samael Janus had held Keri and the children hostage in his *other* life. If the dream was a premonition of what was to come, there was still almost a month before the crash would take place—plenty of time to worry about that later. But how could he know if the dates were accurate? All it would take was one small change in his *other* life to alter the dates in his current reality, resulting in a corresponding date change on the granite markers. Once he saw Keri's face, the depressing thoughts in his dream, along with the demons of death, would disappear.

The jet started its descent for landing at John Wayne Airport. He would need to change into his uniform before leaving the airport, as Keri expected him to be returning from Maui.

As the jet touched down, the vision of facing Keri with the truth was unbearable; he couldn't do it...not now. He decided to wait until after Mother's Day before confessing to Keri, allowing time to pass and life to return to normal.

No reason to rush into it.

Hopefully he could build a reserve of creditability before unloading the bad news. Mother's Day would be a great opportunity for him to express his love to her for her many sacrificial years as an amazing mother and wife. His decision gave him some relief from the pressing stress.

John taxied the jet to Signature Aviation. Michael exited the cockpit and lowered the stairs, eager to get the jet fueled and ready for the return trip to Atlanta.

At the bottom of the stairs John told Ryan, "Don't forget what I said."

Ryan hesitated, trying to remember what John had told him.

"Check your calendar and get back with me, and we will set up a time for you to come over and visit. I want you to meet the rest of the family."

"Of course...I'll get on that first thing," he lied. He would have to see how things went after Mother's Day before he would know if a trip to Buckhead was doable.

"If you need anything, call me. Angel said she hoped you would stay long enough to spend a few days at our beach house. She thought it would do you good."

Wow! They have a beach house, too.

"Sounds like a good plan. I'll give you a call after Mother's Day and let you know."

John laughed. "Mother's Day? How about Father's Day?"

John was right. He would need to confess to Keri before calling. John's suggestion of calling before Father's Day would give him more time—which he needed. "Yeah...I'll be sure to call before Father's Day."

"Great!"

"Talk soon," Ryan said, extending his hand. John ignored his offer to shake hands and reached his arms around Ryan and hugged him.

After a longer than normal hug, John pulled back. "Remember...anything...don't hesitate to call me. We are here for you."

"Right. Thank you. I'll call soon."

What was that all about?

The hug felt a bit mushy, but in an unexplainable way, comforting. It was nice to know that John considered him part of the family.

He made a quick stop in the men's room inside Signature to change into his airline uniform.

Driving away, he saw the Gulfstream taxiing for takeoff.

Hardly remembering the drive home, his mind was wrapped around making the transition from deceptive liar to trusting husband—or at least attempting to appear to Keri that everything was as it should be.

Normally, he would be anxious to see Keri and hold her in his arms, but this time it might be better if she were not home when he arrived. He could use the time to collect his thoughts.

He rolled into the garage and saw her car. Before going inside he checked the mailbox, finding it stuffed with mail. He then noticed the Sunday edition of the Orange County Register rolled up in the driveway.

He took the pile of mail and newspaper into the house and placed it on the kitchen counter. The house was deathly quiet.

"I'm home!"

He was not surprised when no one answered. On a Sunday afternoon, the kids were probably with friends and Keri could have taken a walk.

Before he turned to walk away, he unrolled the newspaper to check the front page headline. It was not the headline that caught his attention, but the date: Sunday, June 8, 2003.

Blood drained from his head and his heart raced. It was June, not May.

How is that possible?

The dream he had at the DoubleTree that morning, before leaving Georgia, must have pushed him six weeks into the future.

How did I go all day and fail to realize it was not Sunday, April 27th, but instead Sunday, June 8th.

He opened his suitcase and pulled out the statement from the DoubleTree.

I never noticed the date, but there it is: June 8, 2003.

No wonder John laughed at him when he said he would call him after Mother's Day.

Mother's Day has already passed! Father's day is next weekend. He must have thought I was crazy!

He tried to replay everything that had happened since he left the hotel at noon.

Something else John had said sounded a bit funny at the time: "Angel said she hoped you would stay long enough to spend a few days at our beach house. She thought it would do you good."

Do me good?

All day long, John never mentioned Keri's name when referring to inviting them back to Georgia to meet his wife and family.

He looked around the kitchen. Everything was put away. He opened the refrigerator. There was hardly anything there. He ran around the house looking for signs to disprove his growing fears. The house looked undisturbed, as if their family had just returned from vacation.

Somehow he had disconnected from reality after waking from his dream at the DoubleTree, but being home—in his house—he slowly reconnected. Nausea stirred in his stomach. The kids were not with friends. Keri was not taking a walk around the block.

John's caring embrace as he said good-by at the airport, and his comment: 'She thought it would do you good.'

He suddenly realized the reason for his unexplainable loneliness, his hollow depression, his troubled spirit, and the sense he was frozen and cut off from the world of the living.

The dream he had in Georgia at the DoubleTree had defined the reality that Keri, David, and Martha were dead. The trip he had made to Georgia was not to find Angel, but to bury his family.

CHAPTER 33

Southern California
Sunday evening—June 8, 2003

The longer Ryan was home, the more connected he became with his current reality. Removing his clothes from his suitcase, an envelope dropped to the floor. It was simply addressed: RYAN. He opened it and removed a sympathy card.

> *Life so fragile, loss so sudden, heart so broken... In the wake of such a loss, we are haunted by things we don't, and may never understand. Yet the solace we seek may not come from answers. So we look for comfort in the belief of love's everlasting connection. May that love lift you and hold you close, and give you peace.*

Beneath the message were the handwritten words…

> *Our deepest sympathy during your time of loss. Please know we are here for you.*

With Love,
John, Mercy, Michael, Susan and
Ronald.

The card had been placed next to his seat in the cabin of the Gulfstream on his flight to Atlanta Friday the sixth of June.

The house was eerily quiet with only a ghostly remembrance of Keri and the children. Just ten days ago, the sick, deranged lunatic—Samael Janus—murdered his family. There had been no formal ceremony; only a quiet graveside remembrance at Oakland Cemetery, attended by Ryan, John, and Michael. Rex offered to be there to show his support, but Ryan discouraged him from making the trip.

When he called John on Friday morning—June 6th, the week after the tragedy—although John was spending the week with his family at the beach, he insisted he fly out to California—instead of dispatching another plane.

He and Michael departed from Panama City, Florida, and flew direct to John Wayne Airport on Friday afternoon. Ryan was waiting when they landed, and they flew to Atlanta that night. John and Michael accompanied him to the cemetery on Saturday morning.

The grave markers for Keri and the children were located by the MITCHELL/HART tombstone on the MITCHELL side. Markers for Ryan's mother and father were centered in front of the tombstone. Keri had mentioned how she wanted her marker to be with the Mitchell family, near Martha Mitchell. Keri's parents, Ronald and Barbara Ann, were buried on the opposite side of the tombstone—the HART side.

Ryan had knelt on the plots where the three markers were installed, opened the three small plastic boxes which contained the cremains of each family member. He tore open the plastic bags within each box, reached in and took a handful of the gray dust from each box and let it fall between his fingers into the grass beside their respective granite markers. He then closed the boxes. He had arranged to have the rest of their cremains properly buried on the gravesite in accordance to Oakland Cemetery's special rules.

John and Michael flew back to Panama City that night to pick up Angel. They had just returned to Peachtree DeKalb Airport on Sunday when Ryan arrived for his trip back to California.

As Ryan had approached the Mercy Flight hangar, the woman he passed driving away in the large Mercedes Benz must have been John's wife—the same woman that he now believed was his Angel.

Seeing John with a Rudolph nose and rosy cheeks made perfect sense, considering he had spent the entire week at the beach.

With each new dream, Ryan began to question what was real and what belonged in his *other,* constantly-changing life. Because of his dream regressions, time had become a jumbled mess in his mind.

He was perplexed why the death of his family had not affected him emotionally like he thought it should. The ugly monster called Grief was very familiar, but for some strange reason, he had not yet shed a single tear, only a general sense of malaise. Grief had ravaged his spirit for months after the death of his mother, but with his family, it was not the same. Perhaps he was in denial or shock, or even worse—losing his mind.

He needed closure. He needed to return to the grave site again. He would call John on Monday and accept his invitation to return for a visit. After he visited Oakland Cemetery and saw their names etched in the stone and touched the ground where their ashes had become one with the earth, maybe then he would believe it.

Although Keri was dead, if John's wife, Mercy, was in

fact *his* Angel, a final dream regression—the seventh dream—might give him one last opportunity to make choices that could turn his present painful reality into tomorrow's *other* life—bringing Keri, David, and Martha back.

CHAPTER 34

Atlanta, Georgia
Friday afternoon—June 13, 2003

*R*yan's spirit lifted when he heard John's voice on the phone. He and Michael were in Dothan with the family when Ryan called, but John sounded eager to fly out to California and shuttle Ryan back to Georgia to join his family for Father's Day.

After dropping Ryan in Atlanta, John and Michael planned to fly back to Dothan, spend the night, and then return to Atlanta Saturday morning with the entire family.

The Gulfstream touched down at Peachtree DeKalb Airport at three o'clock Friday afternoon and taxied to the Mercy Flight hangar.

John left the cockpit and stepped into the cabin to open the entry door for Ryan. When the door swung open, a hot wave of summer heat overcame the climatically-controlled cabin. The invading humid air rushed in carrying the faint smell of jet fuel.

"Ryan, I'll meet you at the foot of the stairs, but first I need to talk to Michael about the fuel load to Dothan." John returned to the cockpit.

Ryan exited the cabin into the sauna-like heat. He squinted up at the gray canopy of thick haze masking the normally-blue sky. To the west, the sky was ominously dark.

Descending the stairs, beads of perspiration began oozing from his pores—the temperature rising with each step closer to the heat-soaked, black asphalt.

Several minutes passed before John finished his business in the cockpit and joined Ryan on the ramp. "Ryan, your car is parked out front...the keys should be in it, and you have a room reserved at the DoubleTree for tonight."

"So you're planning to bring the family back home tomorrow, right?"

"As soon as we get refueled, Michael and I will zip down to Dothan and spend the night with the family. We'll all be back in the morning—should touchdown at approximately ten o'clock. As we discussed earlier, I'll pick you up at the DoubleTree at eleven ."

"John, I hate to be any trouble."

John gave him a hard stare. "What did I tell you when we first met?"

"I know, but..."

"But...nothing. We are thrilled you are here to spend Father's Day with our family. I'm just sorry you have to stay in the DoubleTree tonight. When you called, we were all in Dothan, but now that you are in town, we can easily move the party to Buckhead."

"Well...all I can say is I'm honored. Thank you, and don't worry about me tonight. I'll be fine. Before I go to the hotel, I think I'll drive down to Oakland Cemetery."

John looked at the sky to the west. "Just so you know...on arrival we had to circumnavigate a nasty line of thunderstorms moving in from the west. Depending on traffic, you should have time to make it to the cemetery before the weather hits. I hope you don't get wet."

Ryan held his arms out. "I feel like I'm already soaked."

He laughed. The back of his shirt and underarms were sopping with sweat.

"Welcome to summer in the South."

"Yeah, I'd almost forgotten how hot and humid it gets down here."

"So, I'll swing by and pick you up at eleven tomorrow," John said.

"John, are you sure it wouldn't be easier if you just give me the address where you live and let me meet you at the house?"

"It's no problem. Angel has her car, and I actually have to drive right past the DoubleTree. Plus, I don't want you getting lost looking for the house. We'll leave your car at the hotel and pick it up on Sunday afternoon on the way back to the airport."

Ryan's legs were beginning to sweat. "Okay, I'll be ready at eleven."

The rental car—a full-size Ford sedan—was parked in the same spot as before. He knew he wouldn't be able to sleep until he saw the gravesite. The summer days were long and the sun didn't set until almost nine o'clock. Depending on traffic on I-85 through the city, he should be able to drive to Oakland Cemetery within thirty minutes.

He opened the rear door on the driver's side and put his roller bag on the backseat. He closed the door and then opened the driver's door. When he sat in the driver's seat, he made the mistake of grabbing the hot steering wheel. "Ouch!"

The key was in the ignition. He cranked the car and switched on the air conditioner, adjusting it to MAX COLD. After an initial surge of hot air from the vents, the chilled air began to flow. He closed the driver's door and backed out of the parking space. He was heading south on I-85 within five minutes. For a Friday afternoon, the traffic was not too bad.

After exiting on MLK/STATE CAPITOL, he turned left

onto Oakland Drive and drove 300 feet before turning right into the narrow gate at the main entrance to the cemetery.

Originally named "Atlanta Cemetery", Oakland was founded on six acres of land southeast of the city in 1850. It was the oldest historical plot of land in Atlanta, as William T. Sherman's Union Army burned most of the rest of the city to the ground in 1864 during the Civil War. At the time of the war, Atlanta was a major transportation and medical center for the Southern states, and since several of the largest military hospitals in the area were within a half mile from Oakland, many soldiers who died from their wounds were buried there. In addition, after the war ended, a few thousand fallen soldiers from the Atlanta Campaign, who were previously buried in battleground graves, were moved to the Confederate grounds in Oakland.

During Keri's growing up years, Oakland had been like a museum to her, filled with real-world artifacts from the fictional story she loved so much—*Gone with the Wind*. On her visits to the cemetery, she often recalled episodes in the novel, imagining what it might have been like during that time.

As Ryan navigated the narrow streets inside the cemetery—designed before the automobile—he remembered his many visits to the cemetery with Keri on Saturday and Sunday afternoons while they were in high school; a place they often went just to hang out or have a picnic.

Unlike present-day cemeteries, Victorian cemeteries were referred to as gardens. They were often the only green, manicured location within the city. Families routinely visited relatives on weekends, tended gardens on the family plot, and enjoyed picnics during their visits. Cemeteries of that day were social hubs and a gathering spot for the living, as well as burial places for those who had passed on.

"This is the actual ground where it all happened," Keri once said. "We are walking where families grieved the loss of their fathers, sons, brothers, and husbands who fought for a cause they believed in." However, when referring to the war, Keri agreed with Scarlett O'Hara in saying, "It all seemed like a senseless waste."

The Civil War period fascinated Keri, but Ryan was not sure which came first, her love for history or her love for *Gone with the Wind*. As they walked the grounds, she spoke often of Mitchell's story characters. "If they had been real," she said, "they would have all probably been buried here...like Scarlett's mother and father, Ashley Wilkes' wife, Melanie, Scarlett's two husbands, Charles and Frank, and even little Bonnie, Scarlett and Rhett's daughter—the one who died jumping over the fence on her pony."

Growing up in Atlanta created a special bond with the actual events surrounding the war, not only for Keri, but for most native Atlantans. This connection was greatly solidified beginning in 1936 with Margaret Mitchell's novel—first titled *Tomorrow is Another Day*. The publishers changed the title before publication to *Gone with the Wind*.

Keri found it fitting Margaret Mitchell was buried at Oakland, alongside the almost 7,000 Confederate soldiers that inspired her story—somehow connecting Mitchell to the world that had defined the majority of her short life. And now Keri was buried there too—within a stone's throw of her beloved Margaret.

Once Ronald Hart had become aware of Keri's great love for *Gone with the Wind* and Margaret Mitchell, he contacted the sexton at Oakland Cemetery to locate all of the available plots near the MARSH/MITCHELL gravesite. He negotiated with the owners of plots adjacent to MARSH/MITCHELL and purchased a dozen plots for his family and the family of whoever Keri would marry. Looking back, Ronald Hart knew Keri and Ryan would one day marry, and the fact that Keri would assume the name Mitchell was an added bonus to his masterful plan.

After viewing Ronald Hart's video message in Philip Darby's boardroom back in 1987, Mr. Darby shared with Keri that her father had made certain she, Ryan, and any children they might have would be buried adjacent to Margaret Mitchell. The MITCHELL/HART headstone had already been installed and Ryan's father would be relocated there once Ryan gave the approval—which he did immediately. Martha Mitchell was later buried alongside Ryan's dad, and now Keri, David, and Martha.

Ryan stopped the car on the narrow road beside the brick pathway leading to the Mitchell gravesite. His car blocked the road, but he only intended to stay for a few minutes.

Ryan stepped out of the car. The air felt heavy with pent-up rain, and the temperature was noticeably cooler than when he left the airport—at least ten degrees. Lightening flashed in the distance. He instinctively started counting.

One...two...three...four...five...six...seven...eight.

Thunder boomed.

Knowing sound travels through air at about 1100 to 1200 feet per second, or one mile per five seconds, he calculated the thunderstorm's distance to be less than two miles away.

From the cemetery's elevated position overlooking the skyline of Atlanta, he could see a shadow of darkness had consumed the city.

He hurried up the brick pathway, worn smooth by millions of visitors over hundreds of years. After cresting a small knoll, he noticed a woman standing near the MARSH/MITCHELL gravesite located adjacent to Keri and his family. She wore khaki pants, a white, cotton top, and a wide-brimmed, straw hat with a black ribbon.

CHAPTER 35

Oakland Cemetery
Atlanta, Georgia
Friday afternoon—June 13, 2003

*T*he woman with the wide-brim, straw hat turned and said, "Oh, hello." She stood less than five feet tall and had a noticeably strong, Southern accent. Although the sun was hidden behind darkened skies, she wore sunglasses covering most of her face.

Noticing the woman hovered around the MARSH/MITCHELL plot, he said, "Are you a *Gone with the Wind* fan?"

"I guess you could say I am. How about yourself?"

"I've only seen the movie...never read the book."

She circled the MARSH/MITCHELL plot and stood on the brick path next to him.

"My name is Ryan..."

She cut him off. "Mitchell, I'll bet."

"How did you know?"

"I just assumed, based on the names on these markers. Is this your family—Keri, David, and Martha?"

"Yes."

"How interesting…you are also a Mitchell…and coincidentally located next to Margaret's family. I'll bet that has confused more than one fan."

It's not actually a coincidence…but I'm not going to explain the details to this stranger.

"I'm sure it has," he said.

"Did you know that Margaret's sister-in-law was also named Carrie? Spelled with a C instead of a K."

"Yes, my wife made sure I was aware of that fact, years ago. She was a big fan."

Observing the markers of Ryan's family, she said, "Whatever happened to them? It must have been tragic…all so young and dying at the same time. Was it a car accident? Or perhaps a plane crash?"

Lightning flashed.

One…two…three…four…five…six.

Thunder crashed much louder than before.

The woman said, "Getting closer."

"Yeah…looks like a bad one." The branches of towering oaks and mammoth magnolias stirred the air like mixers, their leaves flashing dark then light with each gust of wind.

Am I dreaming? It feels like a dream.

Ryan answered the woman, "Neither."

"Something much worse?" she said. "Something I assume you had rather not talk about. Am I right?"

"They were murdered."

"Oh my…how dreadful!" She removed her sunglasses and turned to Ryan. Her face had delicate features; her skin was like porcelain. When their eyes met, a calming peace reached deep into his soul. For a moment, he lost interest in the world around him—even his dead family. All he wanted to do was continue staring into the woman's translucent blue eyes. "I'm very sorry for your loss." She hesitated briefly, holding her gaze for at least five to ten seconds before covering her eyes with her large sunglasses.

"Thank you," he said, not knowing if he was thanking her for her kind sentiment or for the peaceful relief he experienced while looking into her eyes—or both.

"The world is crawling with people these days who don't respect anyone or anything. It's not like that where I come from. When did it all change?"

"I'm not sure," he said, still partially dazed from the unexplainable sense of peace he had just experienced.

"Sadly, I'm afraid it will get worse before it gets any better. You know...Evil crouches at our doorstep waiting for the opportunity to rob us of what we need most."

"What might that be?"

"Hope."

"Hope?"

"In the midst of our darkest hour, we must *know* there is hope—a reason to feel that life is still worth living. Just like the city of Atlanta—once burned to the ground, rose out of the ashes to become a diamond of hope for all to see...although in recent years, it has been overcome by Evil's grip."

He stared at the three, granite markers in the grass bearing the names of his family.

How am I supposed to have hope? They're dead.

"Hope is the anchor of the soul," she said, "and without it, we become sick—emotionally, mentally, and sometimes even physically. With hope, a man is capable of bearing incredible burdens while moving forward toward his dreams."

With Keri gone, he was slowly becoming the epitome of hopelessness. He really didn't care if he lived or died—actually, death sounded like the better option.

As though she could read his thoughts, she said, "Ryan, don't lose your hope."

Lightening lit up the sky.

One...two...three.

A blast of thunder made the woman jump.

"Now *that* was close!" she said.

"Yep…less than a mile away."

The leading edge of darkness had moved over the cemetery as the temperature continued to drop. Angry intermittent gusts of wind fought with the limbs of the oaks and magnolias. But even with the approaching rain and danger of lightning, Ryan could not pull himself away from the woman. Something about her made him want to stay and talk…as if she might have answers to his hopelessness.

"You said not to lose my hope…well, you can't lose what you don't have…and to be perfectly honest, I'm a little short on hope these days."

"It's perfectly normal for you to feel the way you do, but don't grieve for Keri or your children—only for yourself. Your family is fine. They are at peace."

"Even though I know that is true, without Keri, my life is meaningless. Everything I did was for her and the children. I have no idea what I will do now."

He had already gone too far, but he felt safe sharing his thoughts with the woman—as he would a close friend. Perhaps being surrounded by death had stripped him of his protective facade of privacy and allowed him to share his personal pains with a stranger.

"Ryan, do you mind if I speak freely?"

"Sure."

"First of all, your life is far from meaningless—even without Keri. God created you for a purpose—something very special that only you can do. Until you discover that purpose, life will be meaningless."

"And I assume hopeless, too."

"When you find your purpose, your hope will return. The two go hand-in-hand."

He stared at the chiseled names in the granite markers. His family was his number one purpose in life, and now they were gone. When they died, they took his hope with them.

"Ryan, how one views hope is best seen in the way they view death? Life is really all about death?"

"Death?"

"How a person views death is the best test of how that person views hope. A person that views death as 'the end' typically hopes in temporal things such as a better job, more money, a nicer house, better health, or even a better world, but that is empty hope. On the other hand, a person that views death as 'a new beginning' will find joy, peace, and strength as the foundation of their hope. Only with an eternal perspective can you have lasting hope."

"I think I understand what you are saying, and I agree we need to think with a bigger perspective, but without Keri, my world is empty—hope or no hope. Now that she is gone, life feels dead to me."

"Ryan, God knew when, where, and how Keri was going to die before she was even born, and He also knew you would be left alone. God is waiting for you."

"Waiting for what? For me to die?"

"No…He is waiting for you to discover your purpose and get busy. You are special to God, and as I said before, He created you for a very specific purpose—as He did everyone on this earth. You can drift through life with one foot in the past and be swallowed up in pity, or you can press on and fulfill your God-given purpose and restore your hope—it's your choice."

Ryan stood silent as he stared at Keri's marker.

She said, "When it comes to your past, wouldn't you say that God has shown you a little bit of mercy?"

"I guess."

"You guess?"

"You act like you know my past," he said.

"I don't need to know your past to know that without God's mercy your life would not be what it is today. Because of mercy, the errors of your past have been erased, as though they never happened."

Her words pulled memories of his past to the surface. There was no doubt that until his family was murdered, God had shown him a lot of mercy. But after that, any compassion God had shown him meant very little.

"Don't let the death of your family rob you of what God has or will do in your life," she said.

It's like she is reading my thoughts. Who is this woman?

She looked up into the sky, the brim of her hat flapping in the wind. "Trust me, there will be many more dark clouds ahead. But God will give you the grace you need to make it through each day, just as He has shown you mercy in regard to your past mistakes."

A strong gust of wind caused the woman to grab her hat, stopping it from blowing off her head.

She continued, "Just as there are dark clouds above us now doesn't mean the bright blue sky is forever gone. This too shall pass. You must keep looking up...beyond this world. If you do, you will find a new strength, a fresh peace, and a lasting hope."

Her words lifted his spirit. Knowing Keri and the children were at peace was satisfying, but for the moment, his grief was the anchor that kept him harbored and unwilling to face seas of uncertainty.

"Grieve as long as you need, but remember...don't grieve for them; they are at peace."

How does she do that? Every time I think something, she acts like she hears it.

Lightning flashed.

One...two.

A crash of thunder followed quickly.

"Wow! We'd better take cover before we get drenched," she said, holding tight to her hat.

Lightning flashed again, followed quickly by a crack and

the rumble of thunder. The storm began not with a sprinkle or drizzle but with a sudden downpour. Torrents of rain fell as though a dam had been breached in the sky.

"I enjoyed talking with you," he said, as he turned and hurried down the brick pathway to his car.

"Me, too," the woman said, moving quickly in the opposite direction holding tight to her hat.

Ryan stopped, forgetting the rain, and called out to the woman, "You never told me your name!"

She called back, "My name is Peggy, but my people call me Hope!"

My people?

By the time he made it to his car, he was soaked down to his socks. He sat in the car sopping wet, while hard-driving rain clattered against the windshield and streamed down the glass. Looking through the distorted lens of water, he searched for Peggy, but she had vanished in the maze of tombstones and mausoleums.

Am I dreaming?

His wet body was all the proof he needed to dispel the thought of being trapped in a dream.

It was like she could read my thoughts...and those eyes...that feeling I had when I looked into her eyes was unreal.

Suddenly, something she had said popped into his head, as if she had sent a follow-up subliminal text message to his brain: "Because of mercy, the errors of your past have been erased, as though they never happened."

Did she mean God's mercy, or was she talking about "Mercy"...John's wife? The woman he now believed to be his Angel from Starbucks?

He started the car and looked out toward Keri's gravesite. He remembered the last line in the note Keri had written him and slipped into his shirt pocket the night she broke up with him on their last date, years ago—the night before he left for the Academy:

> *Promise me that you will never lose hope in tomorrow.*

Hope surged into his spirit with a force more powerful than the deluge that poured over the cemetery. He smiled. "Keri, hang on...I'm coming."

CHAPTER 36

Buckhead, Georgia
Saturday morning—June 14, 2003

Ryan waited in the lobby for John. At exactly 11:00 a.m. his black Lexus pulled under the awning at the DoubleTree.

"How was your flight to Dothan," Ryan said.

"I thought about you after we took off."

"Are you talking about the storm?"

"Yes, what a monster! The line extended as far south as Montgomery. Did you make it to the cemetery before the bottom dropped out?"

"Yeah...barely. I had about thirty minutes before I got drenched."

As they talked, Ryan noticed John had turned from Peachtree onto West Paces Ferry headed in the direction of one of the city's most prestigious residential areas. With impressive mansions—including the Governor of Georgia—and gently curving streets lined with giant, oak trees, the area boasts picturesque Southern charm and a quiet elegance that stood apart from the bustling Uptown neighborhoods only minutes away.

"Do you live down here?" Ryan said.

"It's not too far. We should be home in less than ten minutes. Like I told you, I drive right by the DoubleTree on my way from the airport."

Ryan knew the area well. If John lived "not too far" from where they were, he, no doubt, lived in a mansion. All the homes on West Paces Ferry started at over a million and went as high as twenty million, and those on the side streets were just as pricy. Keri grew up a few blocks from their location on Habersham Road. Pace Academy, where she and Ryan had first met and where all the elite send their children, was only minutes away.

How can he afford to live in this neighborhood?

Sitting quietly, he waited to see if John would turn into a gated driveway of one of the mega-homes on Paces Ferry or head down one of the side streets. Just as Ryan spotted the street sign for Habersham, John slowed and turned.

"Do you live on Habersham?"

"Ryan, do you remember where Mr. Hart lived?"

"Of course I do. It's right there…."

John slowed and turned into the driveway of Keri's old family home. Ryan looked over at John. "Don't tell me…"

"Yep…welcome home."

"How is this possible?"

"All a part of Mr. Hart's plan. Mercy Flight, Inc. owns the house, and we live here rent free."

"Unbelievable. I can't wait to hear this story."

John rolled through the open, iron gate and up the long drive that cut across a perfectly manicured lawn beneath towering oaks and magnolias. He maneuvered the Lexus around the circular drive and parked in front of the house. "I'll explain more later, but first, let's go inside and I'll introduce you to the family."

Exiting the car, Ryan noticed a large, four-door Mercedes sedan parked in the garage. It was presumably the same car he had passed on his way to the Mercy Flight hangar, and more-than-likely, the same Mercedes he had seen Angel driving at Starbucks—something he would know for certain in a matter of minutes.

Ryan followed John into the massive foyer. "Honey, we're home!" John called out. "I want you to come meet Ryan."

He heard footsteps on the hardwood floor leading from the kitchen just before John's wife, Mercy, appeared.

John said, "Honey, I want you to meet Ryan Mitchell."

CHAPTER 37

Buckhead, Georgia
Saturday morning—June 14, 2003

*R*yan's heart skipped and sputtered then jolted into overdrive, pumping blood through his veins like a race horse in the final stretch at Churchill Downs.

It's her! It's my Angel!

His ears grew hot. His throat tightened; the part of his brain responsible for speech froze.

What do I say? Do I tell her how excited I am to finally find her? Do I hug her, thank her, and tell her how desperately I need her to send me back in time so I can change things—make everything right?

As she approached, her eyes offered the welcomed look of a close friend he'd not seen for some time. She extended her hand and said, "Ryan...yes! I remember you from Starbucks. You're the one who asked me about my perfume."

"Oh...yeah...that's right, now I remember," he said, trying to contain any embarrassing outburst of exuberance. He took her extended hand. "Nice to meet you," he said, holding back his many questions...like caged animals in his mind, clawing at his emotions to be unleashed.

He stepped close and instinctively inhaled deeply, searching for the sweet fragrance of the familiar *Angel* perfume.

Nothing.

"What a coincidence," John said. "How nice you two have already met."

"Yes, and I'll never forget how Ryan was the perfect gentleman," she said. "When he first saw me with my tray of coffees, he literally rushed to open the door for me."

John said, "We all look forward to our weekend coffee, don't we, dear? It's something we do when the family is together...sort of a tradition."

'When the family is together.' Now it all makes sense! When I first met her, she said her relatives were visiting from Alabama.

At that moment, the rest of the family entered the foyer. "Ryan, you know Michael," John said. "And this is my daughter, Susan, and her husband, Ronald."

"Yes, I know Michael." He shook Michael's hand. "Nice to meet you, Susan...and Ronald." He shook their hands.

"Ryan," Mercy said, "we are happy you joined us for Father's Day." Empathy formed on her face. "We are also very sorry for your loss and want you to know how much we love you. You are like family to us."

"Thank you, Mercy..."

"Call me Angel."

"Certainly...Angel."

Angel said, "Consider our home your home, and don't hesitate to ask for anything...and I mean *anything*."

"We've already covered that rule," John said. "I think Ryan understands."

"Yes, John has made certain I understand the meaning of 'anything'."

As the shock of meeting Angel began to subside, memories flooded into his thoughts—memories of when he and Keri stood in the exact same spot where he stood. He glanced at the stairway. He imagined her coming down the stairs, wearing something cute, her hair rolled, and a smile stretching from ear to ear. He was always a little nervous at the first sight of her, cherishing every minute they had together, and never wanting their dates to end.

The master bedroom where Ronald and Barbara slept was on the first floor. Keri had the entire upstairs to herself— more than three thousand square feet.

"Michael, come help me grab the bags from the car," John said.

Ryan moved toward the door.

"No, you stay here," John said. "Angel, take Ryan to the kitchen and see if you can find him something cold to drink. I'm sure he is parched."

"Sounds like a great idea," she said. Angel took Ryan by the hand. "Come with me."

The large kitchen had been remodeled since he had last seen it—many years ago, but it still had a certain familiarity that brought back more memories.

"Would like some green tea lemonade?" she said. "I have a special recipe we all love."

"Sounds good."

Angel filled a red kettle with water and put it on the stove. "I think you'll like it. Have a seat. It'll only take a minute to make."

He watched her move about the kitchen with grace and ease. She took a box of tea bags and a jar of honey from the pantry, pulled two glasses and a small pitcher from the cabinet, and four lemons from the refrigerator. When the kettle whistled, she flipped off the eye on the stove. She then filled the pitcher with hot water, hung four tea bags on the rim, squeezed the juice from four lemons in the water— adding the lemon slices—then stirred honey into the mixture.

While the tea steeped, she added ice cubes to the glasses. She then filled the glasses with tea.

"There you go," she said, handing him a chilled glass of tea.

He took a sip. "Very good...not too sweet. I like it."

"I thought you would." She joined him at the kitchen table.

Since he had last seen Angel, he had grown to know her in ways she was not aware—in ways that could only be the work of a masterful dream maker. Although she had never spoken with him outside of their two casual encounters at Starbucks, she had been very outspoken in his dream at Oakland Cemetery in Atlanta where he first saw the grave markers of Keri, David, and Martha.

As he stood in shock, staring at the markers of his beloved family, she had said, "There can be no growth in your life without change. And there is no change without loss. There is no loss without pain."

Ever since, it puzzled him how such words originated from his thoughts, as all thoughts do within dreams.

Sitting across from him at the table, she smiled and said, "It looks like you are deep in thought."

"Do you mind if I ask you a personal question?"

"Fire away...we're family," she said, taking a sip of tea.

"When you think of your past, do you ever wish you could go back and change anything?"

"Let me see..." She twisted her lips to the side as she thought. "There might be a few things, but to be honest, I personally try to let go of the past. I don't mean the good memories; those are what define our lives. I'm talking more about our regrets—the things we wish never happened. We can surely learn from our past mistakes, but holding on to them, letting them simmer in our hearts, will only rob us of our hope."

Her words! They are the same words from my dream!

How is that possible?

She continued. "And without hope...well...life simply feels dead...don't you think?"

"Definitely."

"I think we would all be better off if we spent more time focusing on the present. Each day has more than enough to keep us busy without fretting about the past or worrying about what hasn't even happened."

How did these thoughts of hers get into my dream?

She said, "But I'll admit, it's not easy letting go. For some strange reason, humans tend to find pleasure wading in the pool of 'What if'...even when they know it is filled with hope-eating piranha."

"That's an interesting way to look at it."

"The way I see it, the journey of life is all about the ending. The choices we make every day determine what the story will look like in the end."

Déjà vu. I must ask her...

But before he delivered the question, the sound of the front door closed. "Ryan!" John called from the foyer. Within seconds, he stepped into the kitchen. "Let me show you where you will be sleeping."

"I hope you don't mind," Angel said, "but we planned to put you in Keri's old bedroom."

"That's fine."

She touched his hand and said, "Welcome home."

CHAPTER 38

Buckhead, Georgia
Saturday afternoon—June 14, 2003

Ryan crossed the threshold into—what he knew only as—"Keri's bedroom"; stepping through a crack in time—one foot in the present, the other in a life long ago.

Though the bed was in the same location, the furniture was different. Two windows faced the front of the house towards Habersham Road.

"Take your time," John said, "but when you're ready come join us. We have sandwiches for lunch."

"Thanks, John. I'll be down in a minute."

When John left the room, Ryan sensed a strange oneness with Keri; not the grownup Keri, but Keri, the little girl. He stood in her sanctuary of dreams—the place where she formed her first thoughts of what her life might become one day.

Grief tugged at his heart. His chest tightened. The little girl—who once wrote in her diary, hung memories on her bulletin board, talked with her girlfriends about the boy at school who made her blush, and saw nothing but a bright future ahead of her—was now dead.

He walked to the window and peered down at the circular drive. His mind traveled back to June, 23, 1974; a Saturday evening. By that time, the little girl had grown up. She had graduated from high school that year and was now a beautiful, young lady. It was the last night before her boyfriend whom she had dreamed of spending the rest of her life with was going away to the Naval Academy. The thought of not seeing him—possibly losing him forever—must have torn at her heart.

Salty tears burned his eyes.

Keri, I'm so sorry...

When Ryan parked his '65 Impala on the circular drive that night, he was not prepared for what would soon happen. Unbeknownst to him, only moments before he had arrived at the Hart's house, Barbara Ann had insisted that Keri say her final good-byes to Ryan Mitchell and put an end to their relationship.

He imagined Keri hearing his car arrive, the car door close, and the doorbell ring. The room that had once been her sanctuary of dreams had become her Tower—a prison of holding until the final blow of her words could be delivered to her unsuspecting prey: "I think we need to break up."

After that night, the journey of her life had taken her far from her little-girl dreams and tested her resolve to hold true to her ultimate prince. But in a time of weakness, she had slipped and been lured from her storybook path and into a dark world where the heart is forever scarred.

I am sorry, Keri. I could have stopped it. It was my fault. If only I had made different choices.

Over the years, Ryan had relived every minute of that horrible night thousands of times; from the moment he saw her coming down the stairs, to the moment she had left him sitting alone in his car in the circular drive—in disbelief. Being back in the place where it all occurred had opened old wounds that had long since been covered by the scars of time.

As a child, he had been a victim of Barbara Ann's masterful manipulation, but as an adult, he had no doubts he could easily subvert her scheme—if only he had a second chance.

Angel had apparently not worn her perfume today; hopefully she still used it. Time was running out. In less than twenty-four hours, he would be on the Gulfstream headed back to California.

Perhaps if he mentioned to Angel how wonderful the fragrance was and how he missed smelling it since Keri's death, she might be encouraged to put some on. If not, once everyone had gone to bed, he could spray it on her while she slept. He could sneak into her bedroom and pump a few squirts on her arm, or any other exposed skin, inhale the fragrance, and slip back into his bedroom before he broke into one of his noisy, allergic reactions.

First, he needed to locate her *Angel*. During lunch, he would ask for directions to the nearest bathroom, knowing he would be directed to the half bath off the foyer. But instead of going to the guest bathroom, he would hurry down the hall to the master bath located at the other end of the house. If they happened to find him snooping in their private quarters, he would tell them he got lost looking for the guest powder room. His stomach churned as he contemplated the plan.

Leaving Keri's bedroom, he returned to the kitchen finding Angel alone, putting the last touches on the decorations for a Father's Day celebration—streamers, crepe paper garlands, balloons, and a festive paper tablecloth.

"Happy pre-Father's Day!" Angel said. "We like to make it a two-day affair.

Ryan stopped in the doorway. He was no longer a father—his children were dead.

Angel quickly realized her mistake. "Ryan…I am so sorry; how stupid of me!"

"No, it's fine…"

"It's not fine. I wasn't thinking." She ripped down the streamers hanging in the doorway.

Ryan grabbed her hand. "I promise…I'm fine. It's just the first time I've realized I'm no longer…" Tears spilled from his eyes. "…a father."

Angel handed him a napkin and put her arm around his shoulder. "We don't have to do this. I know everyone would agree."

"No…really…I want you to celebrate. I want you to do everything you normally do. It would be wrong if you didn't. John is a wonderful father and he needs to be reminded of that. I'll be fine. Actually, today will be the perfect time for me to remember all the great memories of my children."

"Are you sure?"

'…don't grieve for them; they are at peace.'

He hesitated, digesting his thought.

"I'm absolutely positive. And as you said earlier, life is all about choices, right? So I'm going to choose to move on with life; think of it as a new beginning. I know it's what Keri would want me to do."

"She certainly would."

Angel positioned herself in front of him. When their eyes met, he instantly felt a calming peace reach deep into his soul. The sensation was identical to what he had experienced at the cemetery when he looked into the translucent eyes of the little woman named Peggy—who called herself Hope. Just as before, he lost interest in the world around him—even his dead family. All he wanted to do was continue staring into Angel's eyes.

"Ryan, how a person views death is a test of how they view hope. By your making the choice to view death as a new beginning, you are certain to find joy, peace, and strength—and a new hope."

Where have I heard that?

"God knew when, where, and how Keri, David, and Martha were going to leave this world before they were even born, and He also knew that you would be left alone."

Peggy...the cemetery...she said the exact same words!

"In the midst of our darkest hour, we must *know* there is hope—a reason to feel that life is still worth living. Just like the city of Atlanta—once burned to the ground, rose out of the ashes."

Peggy said that, too.

"I don't know how this is possible, but everything you just said was verbatim to what a woman said to me yesterday at the cemetery."

"That's interesting. I guess the woman and I must think alike."

Angel turned away. The peaceful bliss he experienced left him—as if she had cast a spell on him and it had now been lifted.

"Honey, I'm starved," John said as he entered the kitchen. "Susan and Ronald are right behind me."

Ryan had not noticed the spread of meats, cheeses, breads, and assorted condiments.

"Perfect timing...lunch is served," she said, pointing to the counter. "Grab a plate and help yourself."

Susan and Ronald joined them and everyone prepared their sandwiches and took a seat at the table. After John said a blessing, Ryan asked Angel, "Could you point me in the direction of your nearest bathroom."

"Just around the corner...you can't miss it."

"Thanks." He stood. "Everyone, please excuse me."

The house had been completely remodeled, but the basic floor plan had not changed. The master suite was at the other end of the house, so he needed to be quick, being careful to walk softly on the hardwood floors. Thankfully, he was wearing tennis shoes.

CHAPTER 39

Buckhead, Georgia
Saturday afternoon—June 14, 2003

On his way to the master suite, he stopped briefly at the guest bathroom, opened the door, then pulled it firmly closed. The sound of the door closing created an audible illusion sufficient for those in the nearby kitchen to believe he had arrived at his destination. He continued quietly down the hallway to the master suite.

He entered the large bathroom with double sinks, a Jacuzzi tub, separate shower, toilet room, and an adjoining, oversized his-and-hers closet. The sink against the far wall obviously belonged to Angel. It was slightly lower with an assortment of female paraphernalia, but no star-shaped dispenser of *Angel* perfume. He searched the medicine cabinet and drawers.

Nothing.

He stepped into her closet and flipped on the light. There was a large built-in makeup vanity, but no *Angel* perfume. He checked the drawers.

Nothing.

If he stayed any longer they might begin to miss him—yet worse…send someone to the guest powder room to check on him.

He rushed out of the bedroom and down the hall, stopping to open and close the powder room door, then into the kitchen. Slightly winded, but not noticeably so, he took a sip of water.

"While you were in the bathroom," Angel said, "we were wondering if you might like to do anything special today."

The only thing he could think of doing was going to the mall and buying some *Angel* perfume. Without it, there was no chance of a final, and most important, dream regression. Angel had once mentioned Macy's in Lenox Square Mall.

He leaned over and whispered in Angel's ear. "I would really like to go to the mall and buy John a Father's Day card."

She looked at him and smiled. "Great idea."

"What's the secret?" John said.

"Ryan and I need to run an errand after lunch. It's a surprise."

Angel backed the big Mercedes out of the garage, shifted into DRIVE, then eased down the long driveway.

Once they arrived at the mall, he would need to go to Macy's alone. He could excuse himself to find the men's room, telling her he would meet up with her at the card racks. While she read Father's Day sentiments, he would be purchasing *Angel* perfume at cosmetic counter.

As they pulled out of the driveway and onto Habersham Road, another idea popped into his head. After buying a card for John, he would take her to the cosmetic counter and encourage her to use the samples of *Angel*. He could tell her how the fragrance reminded him of Keri and how much he missed it.

How could she refuse?

He was certain to burst into an allergic reaction after ingesting the fragrance. Having never witnessed one of his attacks, she would rush him home. He would then excuse himself to Keri's bedroom and hopefully dream one last dream.

When she arrived at the intersection of Habersham and West Paces Ferry, she turned right, drove five blocks—passing the Atlanta History Center on the right. As she approached the traffic light at Peachtree Road, he was surprised when she eased into the far right lane.

"Isn't Lenox Square to the left?" he said.

"Yes, but on a Saturday before Father's Day, it will be a nightmare. The traffic around Lenox and Phipps Plaza is bad enough without it being a holiday weekend."

Oh no! This is not good.

"So where did you have in mind?"

When the traffic light turned green, she wheeled the big Mercedes in a right turn and headed south on Peachtree.

"Barnes and Noble has a great selection of cards. It's much easier."

I'm not looking for easy…I'm looking for perfume.

They drove two blocks, passing Pharr Road where he and Keri had lived in his *other* life after moving back to Buckhead from California.

Angel pulled into the shopping center just past Pharr and parked in front of Barnes and Noble.

"Isn't that the Starbucks where you and I first met?" he said.

"That's it. Fantastic group of employees. I always go there for our weekend coffee."

He had come full circle. The condo complex on Pharr Circle where they had lived—The Habersham Estate

Condominiums—was located behind the shopping center; close enough he often walked to the Starbucks.

It feels like I have lived here my entire life.

Angel waved at a man standing in front of Starbucks wearing a green apron. "That's the manager. He's been at that store forever. I don't think he will ever leave."

"His name wouldn't happen to be Lewis, would it?"

She looked surprised. "Do you know him?"

"We met once when I was in the store."

It makes sense now why Lewis was not able to help me locate Angel. The person I know as Angel, Lewis knows as Mercy.

Unlike Mother's Day, when the selection of cards is normally good up until the last day, the Father's Day section had been picked over.

Ryan started pulling cards and reading sentiments. He hadn't planned on buying John a card, so anything would do. He was so desperate to get his hands on some *Angel* perfume, he considered the possibility of searching the magazines for a scratch and sniff sticker. Even if he did find one, it would be impossible to transfer the fragrance from the magazine page onto Angel's body—especially while she slept.

"See anything you like?" she said.

"Not yet."

Just pick one—anything.

The front of the next card he pulled from the rack read simply: *HAPPY FATHER'S DAY*. He opened the card.

A Dad is patient, helpful and strong
He is there by your side when things go wrong.
He's someone who guides you to do the right thing
And helps you solve problems that life sometimes brings.

That'll do.

He would tell John how much he appreciated him being there for him, helping him solve some of his problems—almost like a father.

Angel walked over. "Find something?"

"I think I'll take this one." He handed her the card.

After reading the sentiment, she said, "That is a *very* powerful message; something we all need to read, not just fathers."

Ryan read the sentiment again, but even after reading it a second time, he was not sure what she saw in the poem that was so special. "What were you thinking?"

"I believe the author of this poem intended for the three words—patient, helpful, and strong—to point us to the past, present, and future. A father is patient, even to the point of allowing his child to make mistakes. *'Things that go wrong'* would refer to the past. The father is helpful to his child every day, working with him to solve problems that might seem unsolvable to the child. *'Do the right thing'* would refer to the present. The father is strong, always standing by his child's side, guiding him toward truth. *'That life sometimes brings'* would be referring to the future. I see it as a message of how a father is there for his child in the past, the present, and the future."

"That is amazing how you read so deeply into that poem. Hearing you explain it gives it a whole new meaning."

"Good choice," she said. "I think John will love it." She showed him her card. "I already bought John a card, but I couldn't let this one go."

The front of the card said, THANKS FOR GIVING ME WINGS. A pair of wings was centered on the front. He opened the card.

"It's blank on the inside," she said. "I've got something special I want to write."

"It's the perfect card for a pilot. I think he'll like it."

"See how easy that was? Sure beats the crowded mall on a holiday Saturday."

"Good choice," he lied.

CHAPTER 40

Buckhead, Georgia
Saturday afternoon—June 14, 2003

*D*uring the short drive back to the house, Ryan hopelessly struggled to come up with a solution to his perfume dilemma.

Angel parked the Mercedes on the circular drive in front of the house, and they entered through the front door. John was in the study seated behind a large mahogany desk reading the paper. He motioned to Ryan. "Come join me."

Ryan sat in one of the soft, leather chairs positioned in front of the desk.

Without any preliminaries, John said, "After Gold Street Capital went belly up in their Ponzi scheme, taking with it all of Mr. Hart's *assumed* fortune, Phillip Darby contacted me. He informed me Mercy Flight, Inc. had been spared along with the bulk of Mr. Hart's wealth."

"How was that possible?"

"Shortly before Hart's death, he had established a charitable remainder unitrust, called a CRUT. The CRUT was funded with all but one-fifth of Mr. Hart's entire wealth."

"Why only one-fifth?"

"That was the amount he left to Keri…and you."

"Are you saying the one hundred million he left Keri was only *one-fifth* of what her dad was worth?"

"Yep. He figured you and Keri would be able to live comfortably with a hundred million."

"It would have been more than enough…if Gold Street Capital had not robbed us."

"Ronald Hart had a plan for practically every possible outcome…"

Ryan cut him off. "Except one…the collapse of GSC."

"Mr. Hart was extremely savvy and very aware of the evil that runs rampant in corporate America. His plan considered every possibility…*even* what happened at GSC."

"How?"

"The CRUT was set up to pay Hart an annual amount until he died. At his death, the law required that the balance remaining in the CRUT must be distributed to a charity. Hart knew he didn't have long to live. He also knew that, by law, upon his death, the assets held within the CRUT would be distributed to his designated charity—which happened to be Mercy Flight, Inc."

"If I understand what you are saying, Mr. Hart put almost his entire estate into a CRUT which was distributed to Mercy Flight, Inc. when he died."

"That's exactly what I'm saying. He carved out enough for Keri and then put the rest into the CRUT. He didn't plan on the Ponzi scheme happening, but he prepared for everything."

"Everything but Keri's death," Ryan said.

"Mr. Hart intended for you and Keri to be appointed as executives in his nonprofit corporation. As execs, you both would receive a salary and benefits. Even though Keri is gone, you are still entitled to the position…which I hope you will consider. Based on the net worth of Mercy Flight, Inc. being nearly a billion dollars..."

"Wait! Did you say a *billion*! With a 'b'?"

"Yes, plus or minus a few million."

"But I thought you said it was four-fifths of his wealth. That would equal four hundred million, not a billion."

"That was the original amount. It has since grown and continues to grow faster than we can spend it. And based on that amount, as an exec, you will be paid a nice base salary plus benefits."

I must be dreaming again.

"That is amazing!"

"Yes, we are all blessed that Mercy Flight is well funded for the future, and we hope you will join us."

Attempting to process John's offer had momentarily distracted him from his number one concern in life of wanting to return to that Saturday night—June 23, 1974. As amazing as the offer was, he would gladly give it all up for one last chance to get Keri back—even if it meant he chanced losing it all and living out the rest of his life in poverty.

He had nothing to lose by accepting John's offer. As things stood now, the chance of another dream regression was not looking too good—unless Angel surprised him and showed up Sunday morning wearing her *Angel* perfume. Not only was Mercy Flight an opportunity of a lifetime, it would allow him to be a part of a wonderful organization aimed at doing great things for people in need all over the world. Keri would want him to help carry-on her father's legacy. "John, I accept your offer."

"Great!" John stood and shook Ryan's hand, pulling him into a manly hug. "I'm sure Keri would be happy to know you will be continuing the work her father started."

"I'm think so too."

Like the sand in an hourglass, the chance of one last dream regression slowly slipped through his fingers. For some strange reason, it appeared John's wife had abandoned the fragrance. Regardless, there would always be another opportunity in the future. When he returned to California, he would purchase more *Angel* perfume. He could give it to her as a gift or spray some on her while she slept—either way, he would be better prepared on his next trip to Georgia.

The remainder of the evening was a celebration of Ryan's acceptance to join Mercy Flight. All the attention was on him, helping to distract him from his semi-depressed state.

By nine o'clock, the group had run out of energy. Susan and Ronald retired to their suite at one end of the house, John and Angel to the master quarters at the other end of the house, and Ryan to Keri's old bedroom upstairs.

After a shower, Ryan read in bed for an hour before turning out the lights. Angel planned to have an early breakfast Sunday morning, celebrate Father's Day, then attend church at Second-Ponce de Leon Baptist Church on the corner of Peachtree and Wesley—located less than a mile from the house. It was the church where Ryan had attended growing up, and was also the church where Keri and her family were long-time members. After lunch, John and Michael would fly him back to California.

His weary mind allowed sleep to come quickly.

CHAPTER 41

Buckhead, Georgia
Sunday morning—June 15, 2003

*R*yan woke from a dreamless sleep, slowly realizing he was in Keri's old family home, in her bedroom. He sunk when he realized—as he did on most mornings—she was gone.

He checked the time—6:07 a.m. He eased out of bed and to the bathroom, relieved himself, splashed water on his face, brushed his teeth, and ran his hand through his hair.

Not expecting anyone to be awake, he slipped on a pair of jeans and a shirt and headed to the kitchen to scrounge up some coffee.

Stepping into the kitchen, he found John and Angel seated at the table drinking coffee. "Good morning," John said, "How did you sleep?"

"Good. How long have you two been up?"

"Angel was up early. She's already made her run to Starbucks. Grab a coffee and join us," John said, pointing to the counter to Ryan's left. He turned and noticed a Grande Starbucks coffee cup. "It's black, so you can fix it the way you like it."

"How nice...thank you." Packets of sweetener, raw sugar, and milk were on the counter.

"It should still be hot," Angel said. "Michael, Susan, and Ronald have already taken theirs."

Ryan removed the white lid from the cup, tore open a sweetener, poured the contents into the cup, and added some milk. After stirring, he replaced the lid and took a sip. The coffee was still hot.

When he sat at the table, he smiled when he recognized the familiar fragrance of *Angel* perfume.

That's it! Thank you Lord!

He drew in a slow, deep breath. He happened to glance at Angel as he released the breath. She smiled, as if she knew what was about to take place.

"Ahhhh...chooo!"

"Bless you," Angel said. "It must be my perfume." She smiled again, as though she were saying *you're welcome.*

"Ahhh...choo!" His nose began dripping and his eyes started to burn. He wiped the water from his eyes and looked at Angel. Words were not necessary. Her eyes said it all. The same peace he had felt before—at the cemetery with the strange woman, and with Angel earlier that day—returned, except this time it was much stronger. John sat quietly and calmly watched, apparently aware of what was about to happen.

"Ryan, why don't you go lie down and see if it will pass," Angel said.

How does she know?

"Good idea," he said, as he stood.

"Go to our bedroom. I just changed the sheets and it will be quieter there," Angel said. "Keri's bedroom is on the front of the house and can be a bit noisy."

Before leaving the kitchen, he turned and looked at John and Angel sitting at the kitchen table, both gazing at him like two statues. Without a reason, he said, "Thank you both for all you have done." His words were spoken as would be a final farewell.

They did not respond, but continued to stare with half smiles, sitting motionless like two ethereal beings. If they had vaporized into a diaphanous mist, he would not have been surprised.

"Ahh...choo!" He hurried down the hall to the master suite. The bed was turned down. Before going to sleep, he went into the bathroom and blew his nose, washed his face, and toweled off.

There it is.

A star-shaped bottle of *Angel* perfume was lying on Angel's vanity. He chuckled. "I wonder where she had that hidden."

An unexplainable happiness lifted his spirit, as if he knew he was about to be rejoined with Keri and his two precious children.

He closed the bedroom door, slipped out of his pants and shirt, and got in bed. With his eyes closed, he imagined Keri's face and her smile.

Keri, I'm coming.

CHAPTER 42

Buckhead, Georgia
Father's Day, Sunday morning—June 15, 2003

I t was June 23, 1974. Ryan and Keri were on their last
date of the summer before he left for the Naval
Academy.

*This is it! The seventh dream. Angel, thank you! You did
it!*

He watched as the scene began to replay in his dream.

"I'm going to miss you," his dream character said, his
back resting against the car door of the 1965 Impala. Keri sat
close to him in the middle of the bench seat.

"I know you'll do great." She took his hand and gently
rubbed it.

Eager to change the ominous outcome he knew was
eminent, he attempted to will words into the mouth of his
dream double. Nothing happened. He was stuck; a spectator
watching a rerun, waiting for the impending tragic scene only
minutes away: *Bambi*: the hunter about to shoot Bambi's
mother; *Titanic*: the supposedly unsinkable cruise ship about
to be gorged by an iceberg; *Romeo and Juliet*: Romeo about

to drink the vial of poison and die beside Juliet's sleeping body.

Wait a minute! It's not supposed to be this way.

His dream double pulled Keri close, kissing her on the forehead. She looked up at him. "Don't cry," he said. He kissed her softly on her lips. "What's wrong? You act like your best friend just died."

Do something you fool before it's too late!

Ryan was lucid, but unable to will his double to speak or act as he commanded in his thoughts.

She snuggled under his arm as they quietly embraced their last intimate moments. "Keri, you know I love you, don't you?"

NO! NO! NO! You must change this!

She sniffed. "Yes," she said, her head still tight against his chest.

He swept a loose strand of hair back behind her ear. She hugged him one more time. Her hand brushed against his chest as she slipped a note into his shirt pocket.

The note! You only have a few seconds!

She looked at him.

I remember this moment. She's about to do it.

"Keri, what's wrong?"

I'll tell you what's wrong! She's gonna dump you in about five seconds if you don't start talking!

She took a breath, exhaling slowly. "Ryan, you're not going to understand what I'm about to say, but I truly believe it is the right thing for you. I don't want anything to get in the way of you reaching your goals. I've thought about it for a long time and...and...I think...." She paused for a moment, then finished it. "I think we need to break up."

"No! Don't say that!"

That's it! Keep after her.

"When you leave, I don't want you to have to think about me," she said.

"How can I *not* think about you?"

"You need to be free."

"But I don't *want* to be free."

"Ryan, the only way I can know if we are truly meant to be together is to let you go."

"But we're *supposed* to be together. Nobody knows you like I do. Nobody sees you like I do. We *belong* together. I love you...I *love* you, Keri. Why are you doing this?"

Come on! You've got to do better than that! Tell her what happens...tell her how she is destroying the future.

"I'm sorry. This is something I have to do, Ryan. I need to date other people."

She's lying! She doesn't mean it!

She opened her door. "I need to go," she said.

"Please don't do this!"

"Ryan, you're going to do great." She got out of the car, closed the door, and didn't look back, hurrying into the darkness.

What were you thinking? STOP HER!!! GO AFTER HER!!!

The sound of footsteps on the pavement, running in the darkness, followed by the door to her house being slammed close.

What! You're just going to sit there? Come on...this is IT! Your last chance!

The dream double sat frozen like a statue. Ryan read his mind—grasping for answers while the sounds of the summer night engulfed him: cicadas and tree crickets.

Go after her!

He started the car, backed out of the driveway, and drove away. The neighborhood streets were quiet.

I'm not believing this! Stop the car! STOP! THE! CAR!

Ryan watched as the dream was on autopilot, replaying the nightmare he had relived for almost forty years.

The note! You need to pull over and read the note!

His dream double pulled the car to the curb, snapped on the overhead light, and pulled the folded note from his pocket.

June 23, 1974

Dear Ryan,

> *I believe if we are meant to be, nothing can keep us apart. As long as I live, I will patiently wait on each sunrise and follow each sunset into tomorrow, for I believe it is the path of the sun that will lead us to our hopes and dreams. Promise me that you will never lose hope in tomorrow.*

I love you,
Keri

Okay, chump...it's make it or break it time. This is your life we are talking about. You MUST go get her...NOW!!!
The dream double sat frozen—again—like a windup doll whose action spring needed a fresh turn of the key.

Ryan noticed three women in the back seat of the Impala. He immediately recognized them all. Behind the driver was Mercy, John Dross's wife—the same woman he now knew to be his Angel from Starbucks. Seated to her right was Grace, the woman that had sold him the *Angel* perfume at the department store in California. And on the far right was the short woman he had spoken with at the cemetery named Peggy—or as *her people* called her, Hope.

Ryan processed the image while his dream double, still frozen in time with the biggest decision in his life before him, was unable to act.

Seated behind the dream dummy, unbeknownst, were

Mercy, Grace, and Hope. Suddenly, everything crystallized in the dim glow of the cabin of his old 1965 Impala.

All of the dream regressions, the meetings with strange characters at coffee houses and cemeteries, and even the illusion of another life had been guided by these three women—Mercy, Grace, and Hope.

Mercy—the woman who had connected him to his dream regressions—had made it possible for him to erase his past.

Grace—the woman who had empowered Mercy with a mystical fragrance.

Hope—the woman at the cemetery who had lifted his spirit beyond the brokenness, suffering and pain, encouraging him he would find peace when his focus was set on things beyond this world.

Look in the rearview mirror you fool! The answers to all your questions are behind you—waiting!

The dreamer responded to Ryan's command and turned his head toward the mirror and stared. The moment his eyes locked on the image in the mirror, three bright beams of light shot out from each woman, joined into one much brighter laser-like projection, struck the rearview mirror and reflected into the wide-eyed dreamer. In a robotic, focused voice, the dream double said, "I can't let her go!"

YES!! Now you're talkin'.

The dreamer reached up and flipped off the overhead light, putting the car in darkness. He hammered the accelerator, spinning the Impala in a U-turn in the street, tires squealing, and raced back to Keri's house. He wheeled into her driveway—his front tires cutting through the manicured grass—parked the car on the circular drive beneath Keri's bedroom window, flung open the car door, and sprinted toward the front door.

YES!

Standing guard, as though she had been expecting him to

return, Barbara Ann opened the door to greet Ryan. "Ryan, did you forget something?"

Don't listen to her. She's the one that messed you up in the first place. Stay focused! Knock her down! Push her to the side! Run through her! Just go to Keri!

"Mrs. Hart, I need to speak with Keri."

"Ryan, darling, perhaps it would be best if you wait until tomorrow."

"No! I need to see her now!" Ryan edged his way past Barbara Ann. "I just need to talk with her a minute."

That's my boy!

Barbara Ann called out as he ran for the stairs, "Ryan, I really think it would be best if you came back tomorrow!"

He ignored her and continued up the stairs and down the hall towards Keri's bedroom.

He slowly opened the door to find her laying on her bed gazing out the window. "Keri…"

She sat up in bed. "Ryan! What are you doing here?"

"I don't believe you." He moved to the side of the bed and sat beside her. "I know you too well. That stunt out there in the car was not for real." He held her hand. "Keri, there might be a lot of things in this world I'm unsure of, but there is one thing I know for certain. We belong together, and you know it."

Beautiful.

She burst into tears, wrapping her arms around him. "Ryan, I love you so much. I'm so sorry. I never wanted to hurt you, but…"

"You don't need to say a word." He pulled her back, held her hands, and looked into her eyes. "Keri, everything is going to work out fine." He gently wiped the tears from her cheek. "I'll do whatever it takes to ensure nothing ever comes between us. If that means not going to the Naval Academy…so be it…that's what I'll do. I love you more than anything in this world. We were meant to be together."

Nicely done.

She sniffled. "But you can't give up your dream."

"Keri, you are my dream...being with you is the only dream I have ever had...I know it now more than ever before. The only dream that haunts me every day is the dream where I lose you."

"No, I can't let you do it." She wiped her wet eyes. "We can write. We won't let anything come between us. I promise. We can make it work, but you must go to the Academy."

Tell her the Academy is off the table. Tell her you have seen the future!

"Listen," he said, "sitting here right now, holding your hands, looking into your eyes, I know there is no place I'd rather be. Tonight has opened my eyes to my greatest fear— losing you. I have seen our future and what will happen if I let you go tonight. I don't want to live with any regrets. Please trust me. I know this is the right thing to do."

Fresh tears spilled from her eyes. She hugged him. "Ryan, I love you."

Sweet.

CHAPTER 43

Buckhead, Georgia
Father's Day, Sunday morning—June 16

R yan looked around the room. He was not in his California bedroom where he had hoped to be. That could only mean one thing...

I'm still in John's house in Georgia?

Nothing had changed since he went to sleep. Everything had been riding on the seventh dream, but sadly, Keri, David, and Martha were still dead, and he was still in Georgia.

I don't understand. I did everything right in the dream. I didn't go to the Academy. Keri and I decided we couldn't live without each other. We were together. It doesn't make sense.

His heart began to race, and for a moment he couldn't breathe. Then suddenly he was breathing shallowly, rapidly, and expelling the same word with each exhalation: "No, no, no, no! God, please, take my life, but let my family live."

Where is Your mercy? Where is Your grace? Where is the hope?

His eyes burned. Unspilled tears clouded his vision. "Why, God, have you done this to me?"

Tears rolled down his cheeks. He drew in deep, sharp breaths. All the pain, grief, and anger—struggling for weeks to break loose of confinement and burst full-born into the world—had finally found freedom.

His heart fought to reject the permanent sense of loss only death can bring. It was clear he would never see Keri and the children again. As he struggled to understand why Angel did not return his family to him, he remembered the words she had spoken to him while he dreamed.

I'm not the one who is going to change things, and contrary to what you think, it's not in your dreams where things are changed. Dreams are worthless unless you wake up and actually act on them. You're not going to change your life until you choose *to change. It's not about the past, it's about the present, and you are stuck because you haven't learned how to let go of the past. You can only learn from the past, holding on to it will only rob you of your hope in the future.*

Tears poured from his eyes. His throat tightened. His chest heaved with grief.

"Why, Lord!"

After several minutes, he wiped his eyes and face, turned and sat on the edge of the bed. After gaining his composure, he stood and headed for the bathroom—then stopped abruptly, realizing the door was not where he expected it to be. He surveyed the room. He was not in Keri's old bedroom, but instead in the master bedroom where John and Angel slept.

They had insisted I take a nap in the master bedroom.

The master bath was familiar, but in some way different. The clutter of female paraphernalia around Angel's vanity had been removed—even the star-shaped bottle of *Angel* perfume he had noticed before was gone.

Angel must have come into the bedroom while I was sleeping.

The area was clean and neat. He peeked into Angel's dressing room. It looked much the same as when he had snooped around searching for the *Angel* perfume.

Seeing John and Angel would not be easy. Seeing them would only confirm his present reality and the mistaken belief things would be different when he woke.

He went to John's vanity, turned the faucet to HOT, took a wash cloth, and began soaking it with warm water. After washing his face, he dried it with a hand towel.

Making his way down the hallway, he heard the buzz of familiar voices in the kitchen. Approaching the kitchen door, the voices grew louder—each voice taking on its own distinct clarity. Michael, Susan, and Ronald had apparently joined John and Angel in the kitchen.

Something doesn't sound right.

Strangely, his heart thumped hard inside his chest. What were the chances he had been zapped into a strange and unfamiliar place—perhaps even a stranger's house. How would he explain to the strangers he, like Goldilocks, had been sleeping in their bed?

He turned the corner and stepped into the kitchen.

"Hi, honey."

"Keri! It's you!"

"Who did you expect?"

He looked around the kitchen. "And David...and Martha! And...Ronald?"

Ronald?

David and Martha were not fifteen-years old, but thirty. His mind raced in thought.

Martha married Darby's son. Of course she did. What was I thinking?

"Is anyone else in the house?"

Keri walked over to him, placed one hand on each cheek, holding his head still and said, "What are you talking about? What did you want me to do, invite the entire neighborhood over for Father's Day?"

His eyes filled with water, tears spilled on his cheeks, he wrapped his arms around her. "I love you, and I'm never letting you out of my sight! Never! Never! Never! You understand?" David, Martha, and Ronald watched and murmured among themselves with occasional chuckles.

With her face smashed tight against his chest, Keri spoke in a muffled voice, "Are you okay? First, you act like you don't know me, then you get all emotional, and now you have me in a death grip as your prisoner. Ryan, I'm not going anywhere. You can let me go now before you suffocate me."

He released her, and then kissed her. "I'm sorry. I got carried away."

She kissed him back. "That's why I love you—always a surprise around every corner. I've just never seen you so excited about Father's Day."

"Oh…that's right! It's Father's Day!"

"Dad, are you okay?" Martha said.

"I've never been better. I'm just happy we are all together."

I don't believe this!

Slowly, he synched with reality, bringing all the big pieces into focus. He was in Georgia where he and Keri had lived their entire lives. They lived in Keri's parent's old home in Buckhead on Habersham Road. The house had been remodeled—actually gutted and rebuilt—before they moved in.

Long ago, after the night in the driveway on June 23, 1974, he had decided not to attend the Naval Academy, but instead to attend college with Keri. Thanks to Ronald Hart offering to finance his education, Ryan had attended Auburn University where he studied Aviation Management. Keri also graduated from Auburn with a degree in nursing.

They had married in June, after graduating from Auburn in May of 1979. Unlike in his *other* life, Barbara Ann had turned out to be a wonderful mother-in-law and grandmother.

Ryan went to work for Ronald Hart as a copilot flying his Gulfstream and became the chief pilot when Ronald formed Mercy Flight, Incorporated.

"Here dad," Martha said. "David and I found the perfect card we wanted to give you. We both liked it so much, we couldn't decide who was going to give it to you, and we didn't think you would want two of the same cards."

The front of the card read simply: *HAPPY FATHER'S DAY*. He opened the card.

Father's Day - 2013

A Dad is patient, helpful and strong
He is there by your side when things go wrong.
He's someone who guides you to do the right thing
And helps you solve problems that life sometimes brings.

We love you,
Martha and David

When he finished reading the card he looked up. Martha said, "I believe the author of this poem intended for the three words—patient, helpful, and strong—to point us to the past, present, and future.

"A father is patient, even to the point of allowing his child to make mistakes. *'Things that go wrong'* would refer to the past.

"The father is helpful to his child every day, working with him to solve problems that might seem unsolvable to the child. *'Do the right thing'* would refer to the present.

"The father is strong, always standing by his child's side, guiding him toward truth. *'That life sometimes brings'* would be referring to the future. I see it as a message of how you have been there for David and me throughout our entire lives, in the past and the present. We know you will also be there for us in the future. We love you."

Wow! Déjà vu. I feel like I've lived this moment before.

"I love you both so very much. Thank you, Martha." He hugged Martha and kissed her forehead. "Thank you, David." He gave David a manly hug.

The twins, David and Martha, were born August 31, 1983, not 1988. David had followed in Ryan's footsteps and obtained an aviation degree from Auburn and then returned to fly for Mercy Flight, Inc.

Martha Mitchell and Ronald Darby were introduced at an early age. They soon became childhood sweethearts, attended Pace Academy in Buckhead, and both graduated from the University of Alabama where Ronald also attended law school—as did his father, Philip Darby. Martha graduated in accounting, and after gaining the required experience, obtained her license as a Certified Public Accountant. Martha oversees the financial side of Mercy Flight, Inc.

Martha and Ronald married after Ronald finished law school. They decided to remain in Alabama and picked Dothan to live because of its friendly community and relatively small size. In addition, it had two large hospitals and scads of physicians and clinics. This was a great asset for Ronald as he specialized in medical malpractice defense representing doctors, physician groups, and clinics throughout Alabama and Georgia. He was also the Chief Legal Counsel for Mercy Flight, Inc.

The Dross family did not exist—except in his *other* life. They were dream characters cast in his thoughts, playing the role of his own life, while he lived out the lessons of his *other* life.

"Here, honey," Keri said. "Read my card."

The front of the card said, THANKS FOR GIVING ME WINGS. A pair of wings was centered on the front. He opened the card.

> *Father's Day*
> *June 16, 2013*
>
> *Dear Ryan,*
>
> *I believe if we are meant to be, nothing can keep us apart. As long as I live, I will patiently wait on each sunrise and follow each sunset into tomorrow, for I believe it is the path of the sun that will lead us to our hopes and dreams. Promise me that you will never lose hope in tomorrow.*
> *Thank you for being my wings as we have journeyed through life together.*
>
> *I love you,*
> *Keri*

His eyes filled with tears. His lips strained. He looked at Keri. "The note."

"Yes, the famous note."

He put his arm around her. "Keri, have you ever imagined what might have happened if I had gone to Annapolis?"

"I think about it all the time. I remember that night like it was yesterday. I can't explain how wonderful it felt when I looked up and saw you waltzing into my bedroom—my Prince Charming."

He kissed her. "I love you more than you will ever know."

"I love you, too. We were meant to be…just as I said in the note."

From Keri's perspective, nothing in Ryan's *other* life

had ever been a part of her reality. Her life started in Buckhead and remained in Buckhead the entire time. Trying to explain his *other* life to her would be impossible. It would always remain in his thoughts as a reminder that everything he had was only because of God's mercy and grace.

None of it ever happened—he never went to the Naval Academy, he never met the crazy Rex Dean, he never met or married the seductive Emily Anderson, and everything that had occurred on that dreadful night, when Evil came knocking at his door, was nothing more than a much-too-real nightmare. It was all a dream.

Looking at his wonderful family, he could only surmise that his dreams had been used to show him how blessed he was and what could have happened if he had made different choices throughout his life—how, so easily, it could have all slipped away.

There was no way to know what stimulated the dreams; perhaps it was the realization of how blessed he was and the horrid thought of losing it all; or perhaps it was due to his great empathy for others as he sensed their pain and suffering, mostly brought on by their bad choices.

One thing was for certain; his dreams had shown him that life was a fragile balance of choices. The only way to avoid creating regretful yesterdays was to place the highest priority on the choices he made today, for his today would soon become tomorrow's yesterday.

THE END

AUTHOR'S NOTE

The three major themes that inspired the final book of the *Flight Trilogy* were choice, purpose, and hope.

CHOICE: When you come to a fork in the road of life, the fork requires you to either make a decision or remain paralyzed by neutrality. One road is wide, smooth, and well-trafficked. The other is narrow, rugged, and lonely. Your choice leads to another fork a little farther down the road, and the decision you make there leads to yet another.

Choices made on the basis of our feelings alone, or on the response of others, usually cause us to regret our decision later. Part of the reason why we make the wrong choice is because we have not yet decided on our worldview—where we stand on matters of character, morality, values, godliness, and commitment to Christ.

In the opening chapter of *Flight to Freedom*, Ryan and Keri are waiting for the movers to arrive. While looking back on the past twenty-nine years of his life, Ryan feels a sense of hopeless regret and wonders what his and Keri's lives might have been like if they had made different choices. He asked Keri, "If you could live your life over, what would you do differently?"

Life teaches us that our God-given capacity to choose is both our greatest blessing and our worst curse. Good choices fill us with satisfaction, happiness, peace, contentment, and joy—creating memories that grow sweeter with time. Bad choices burden us with regret, sadness, sorrow, and heartache—burdens that often grow heavier with time. Collectively, the choices we make throughout our lives shape our personality, form our self image, and ultimately define our future.

Sadly, we cannot go back. We can never reclaim those moments when we were possessed by rage, or lust, or cruelty, or indifference, or insensitivity, or disrespect, or hard-headed pride. We must forever live with the consequences of our words and our actions. The Scriptures warn: *"A man reaps what he sows."* Galatians 6:7 (NIV)

PURPOSE: Thomas Carlyle said, "The man without a purpose is like a ship without a rudder—a waif, a nothing, a no man."

People are shaped by God for a specific purpose. Contrary to what many believe, our dreams of success are not God's purpose for us. In fact, His purpose may be the exact opposite. God's purpose is for this very minute, not for sometime in the future. His purpose is the process itself. Knowing and living God's purpose gives meaning and hope to life, because that is what you were created to do. It is the one thing that will fulfill you and satisfy you above all else.

Before you can discover your purpose, you must first discover the One who designed you for that purpose. *"It's in Christ that we find out who we are and what we are living for. Long before we first heard of Christ and got our hopes up, he had his eye on us, had designs on us for glorious living, part of the overall purpose he is working out in everything and everyone."* Ephesians 1:11-12 (MSG)

HOPE: A man can live approximately thirty days without food, thirty hours without water, and three minutes without air, but a man cannot live without hope. Hopelessness is the greatest problem on the planet.

When life doesn't make sense, we lose our peace, we lose our joy, and we feel hopeless. Hope is restored when we discover God's purpose for our life and realize that His great love for us is greater than any problem we will ever go through. *"I know what I'm doing. I have it all planned out—plans to take care of you, not abandon you, plans to give you the future you hope for."* Jeremiah 29:11 (MSG)

It is my observation that we journey through life on one of three paths:

   1. **INDEPENDENCE:** The path of absolute independence where God is viewed as an inference and theology is indefinite or inadequate, unreliable or unbelievable. On this path destiny relies solely on human intelligence, ability, and chance.
   2. **ACCEPTANCE:** The path of acceptance that God is the Creator of heaven and earth, the Bible is His Word, and the belief that it is only through His Son, Jesus Christ, that man can have eternal life. On this path destiny is an amalgamation of God's love for humanity and man's self-will.
   3. **SURRENDER:** The path of complete surrender to God's sovereignty and belief that each man was created and shaped by God for a specific purpose, and that apart from God's purpose, man is incapable of finding lasting peace and satisfying hope. On this path destiny is believed to be divinely engineered and individually designed by the One who created the heaven and the earth. *"In the beginning God created the heaven and the earth."* Genesis 1:1

God gives us the freedom to decide how we will act and the ability to make moral choices. Our personal *Flight to Freedom* depends on our ability to choose Christ, for it is in Him that real *Freedom* exists. *"So if the Son sets you free, you will be free indeed."* John 8:36 (NIV)

Flight to Freedom

I lay upon my back one day and looked into the sky.
I watched a wispy cloud up high go freely drifting by.
It made me think upon my life, the *choices* I had made.
Might things have turned out differently if only I had prayed?

I wondered if that cloud God made, had been another shape,
Would someone have missed the benefit beneath its shadowed drape?
It made me think upon my life, the years I'd frivolously spent.
If only I'd more clearly known for what *purpose* I was meant.

The cloud was but a vapor made of water and of air.
It drifted along God's chosen path not a worry or a care.
It made me think upon my life, the *hope* that I had lost.
The weight of regret and sorrow, I'd carried at great cost.

I lay upon my back one day and looked into the sky.
I watched a wispy cloud up high go freely drifting by.
It made me think upon my life and God's great love for me.
I suddenly came to realized, only in Him could I be free.

Mike Coe

Made in the USA
Charleston, SC
04 August 2013